LEAVE IT TO THE TOFF

The Hon. Richard Rollison received a legacy—
a country mansion and fifty thousand pounds
—from a man he helped to put behind bars
many years ago. Is this a sign of death-bed
conversion, an example of the virtue of human
forgiveness, or is there a more sinister motive,
a plan of revenge from beyond the grave?

JOHN CREASEY

THE TOFF SERIES

The Toff on Board
Kill the Toff
Fool the Toff
A Knife for the Toff
The Toff Goes Gay
Hunt the Toff
Call the Toff
The Toff Down Under
The Toff at Butlin's
The Toff at the Fair
A Six for the Toff
The Toff and the Deep Blue Sea
The Toff in New York
The Toff on Fire

Model for the Toff
The Toff and the Stolen Tresses
The Toff on the Farm
The Toff and the Runaway Bride
Double for the Toff
The Toff and the Kidnapped Child
A Rocket for the Toff
Follow the Toff
The Toff and the Teds
A Bundle for the Toff
Make-up for the Toff
Leave it to the Toff
A Doll for the Toff
The Toff and the Spider

The Toff in Wax

JOHN CREASEY

LEAVE IT TO
THE TOFF

HODDER AND STOUGHTON

Copyright © 1963 by John Creasey

First printed 1963
Hodder Paperback edition 1967

*Printed in Great Britain
for Hodder and Stoughton Ltd.,
St. Paul's House, Warwick Lane, London, E.C.4,
by Richard Clay (The Chaucer Press), Ltd.,
Bungay, Suffolk*

1

THE LETTER

THE letter was among the twenty-seven which dropped into the wire cage behind the letter box at 22g, Gresham Terrace. They were variously addressed. The wholly correct ones read:

The Hon. Richard Rollison, D.S.O., M.C., M.B.E.

Others, much simpler, simply read *Richard Rollison Esquire*, others shortened the Richard to R, several said bluffly: *Mr Richard Rollison.* Two left out the "i" in Rollison, one had only a casual acquaintance with capital letters, and read *mr rIchard rollyson*, and one—inevitably one in any large batch of mail—simply read:

The Toff, W.1.

Of these, the most intriguing and in its way gratifying was the one which read: *The Toff, London, Eng.* This came from an obscure village in Australia, and invited the Toff to invest in a gold mine, reminding him that he had met the writer near the Great Barrier Reef, eight years or so ago. Rollison put this aside for special consideration later, and skimmed through the others.

There were three begging letters, four notices of committee meetings for charitable organisations, five notes from old friends, several dividend cheques—for this was the end of June—a letter from his Aunt Gloria, then in Italy, announcing that torrential rains were driving her home, and finally one which had a Lincoln's Inn address embossed with the name of a firm of solicitors, Gammon & Hanbury. This read:

5

Dear Sir,

If you will be good enough to call at these offices, preferably by appointment, we believe that you will learn something to your advantage.

Yours very truly

The writing at the foot was indecipherable, but the initials typed at the top of the letter, G.H., suggested that the author might be Mr Hanbury himself. Rollison put this aside, also. As if with second sight, his man Jolly came into the little dining alcove where the Toff breakfasted on those mornings when he had any time to spare.

"Would you like some fresh coffee, sir?"

"Yes," said Rollison. "And while you're getting it, try to remember Algoa Prendergast, will you?"

"Very well, sir."

Jolly, who was in the middle-sixties and on such trouble-free periods as this looked no more than fifty-five, had served the Hon. Richard Rollison for a long time. Rollison was twenty years or so Jolly's junior, but the years had so influenced them that they were much more friends than employer and employed or, as Jolly would put it even in the second half of the twentieth century, than master and man.

Outside, there was a hint of sun and a hint of rain on the roofs at the back of the houses in Gresham Terrace. Inside, there were the odd noises as Jolly put the finishing touches to the coffee. When he brought it in, the Toff spread a lot of butter and even more marmalade on a small piece of toast. Jolly placed the fresh coffee pot on the table.

"Australia, sir," he said.

"Yes."

"The Great Barrier Reef."

"You are not slipping," conceded Rollison.

"Wasn't he the man with the odd eyes?"

"One grey, one blue—yes," confirmed Rollison, and

waved to a chair. Jolly sat down, and poured out two cups of coffee. "And bald-headed, too."

"I recollect that he looked tough enough to wrestle with a shark, and boasted that he had once done so," remembered Jolly. "He took us out to sea in one of the glass-bottomed boats, and some sharks were very close. A somewhat grisly experience."

"Yes," said Rollison. "He wants a thousand pounds."

"Indeed, sir."

"To develop a gold mine which he has discovered in the Northern Territories. He says."

"What does he offer in return, sir?"

"A quarter share in the mine." Rollison handed over the letter from Algoa Prendergast. It was written in a sprawling handwriting on a blue airmail letter form, and was brief and to the point.

"But no other security," remarked Jolly, and sipped his coffee sagely.

"Jolly."

"Sir?"

"Can we spare a thousand pounds?"

"Does he specify sterling or Australian pounds?"

"Most emphatically, he specifies sterling."

"I recall that he had a curious attitude towards the difference in value between the two currencies," mused Jolly.

"Can we?"

"Well, yes, I think we can," conceded Jolly, very thoughtfully. "It would have to come out of the Risk and Hope Account, sir." This was the name which Rollison had recently given to an account which a more prosaic person would have called the Charitable Account, or Loan Fund. There had been a time when he had been in serious financial difficulty, and from then on he had allowed Jolly to charge fees to individuals whom he, Rollison, helped in matters of investigation.

Part of these fees had already gone into the Risk and

Hope account, and these days half of every fee went there. The account was used to help lame dogs over stiles, guide discharged convicts into the final straight, and assist plausible loan-supplicants like Algoa Prendergast to gamble—provided they gambled with their time as well as his money, Rollison felt that such a venture was as good as any.

After a pause, Jolly went on: "When does he require the money?"

"He asked me to send a draft by airmail."

"Taken by and large, sir, I think it would be a reasonable risk," said Jolly. "At the time we knew him he was pearl diving, and hoping for a fortune. He wanted you to finance him if he ever found a profitable bed of oysters or clams, but we didn't hear from him about that."

"Meaning, that you think he's honest when he says he's struck gold."

"I think we can safely assume that he thinks he has."

"Yes," said Rollison. "Yes. We'll sleep on it, and make up our minds in the morning." He pushed the letter from Gammon and Hanbury across the table, and sipped his coffee. "Do you know these people?"

Jolly read both heading and letter, and replied:
"No, sir."

"Ring Grice up, and find out if he knows anything about them, will you?" suggested Rollison. "The address is in Lincoln's Inn; that sounds pretty safe."

"I will make inquiries," promised Jolly, "and if they are satisfactory, shall I make an appointment with you for this morning?"

"Why so soon?" inquired Rollison.

"I did intend to work on the Trophy Wall, sir."

"All right, I'll get out of your way," said Rollison. "If I can't see G. & H., I'll go and talk to the ducks in St James's Park. I like the gorgeous originality of the phrase 'something to my advantage', don't you?"

"It suggests an elderly legal gentleman," said Jolly, as

if it did not occur to him that he himself was a person of any maturity.

Rollison set himself to answer those letters which needed immediate attention, sitting at his large, flat-topped desk with his back to the long Trophy Wall, with its souvenirs of the murder cases in which he had been involved over the years. He heard the ting! of the telephone before Jolly talked to Superintendent Grice, of New Scotland Yard. He kept seeing mental pictures of Algoa Prendergast at the helm of the flat-bottomed boat, bellowing at sharks and squid and jelly-fish, at colourful little fish—and cursing the deceptively sharp beauty of coral.

"*One of these days I'm going to make a fortune,*" Algoa had boomed. "*And if you don't come in with me, you'll be a bigger fool than I thought you were.*"

His letter seemed to be shouting the same sentiments.

* * *

At two minutes to eleven, Rollison stepped out of what must surely be the most antiquated lift in London, and found himself confronted by green painted walls, grey tiled floors, frosted glass windows in dark wooden doors. A sign painted on the wall pointed to the right for Gammon and Hanbury, who had been given a clean bill by Scotland Yard. The door leading to their offices was at the end of a passage, and the word *Inquiries* was there in black.

Rollison stepped inside. A grey-haired woman was bending short-sightedly over a book which looked as if it had been bought in the days of Mr Scrooge. She glanced up, and peered at Rollison with faded, watery eyes. She looked just as old as one would expect from the phrase 'something to your advantage'. Her white silk blouse was spotless, and fastened high at the neck.

"Good morning, sir." She had a faint Irish brogue.

"Good morning. I have an appointment with Mr Hanbury."

"With *whom*?"

"Mr Hanbury."

"Mr *Han*bury," the woman echoed, as if the name was unfamiliar to her.

"Of Gammon and Hanbury."

"Oh, yes," the woman said. "Mr Gammon's in."

There could have been a mistake, although Jolly seldom slipped up.

"May I have your name, please?"

"Rollison," said Rollison.

"*Row*lison?"

"Rollison."

"Mr *Roll*inson."

It wasn't worth fighting about.

"For an eleven o'clock appointment with Mr Hanbury," Rollison affirmed.

The woman's eyes looked troubled and harassed.

"Mr Hanbury," she repeated, with that rather vague and forlorn air. "Mr Gammon's in."

"Isn't Mr Hanbury in?"

"Mr Hanbury's out."

"I made an appointment with him for eleven o'clock."

"Did you?" she inquired, with a sudden flare of interest.

"Yes. About a letter he wrote to me."

"About a *letter*," echoed the grey-haired old woman, and but for her apparent anxiety to please, she would have annoyed Rollison by now. Could anyone be quite so vague? Was she just being awkward, or was she stalling?

As she gazed up at him, footsteps sounded in the passage leading to the office, the quick brisk footsteps of a young male. The door swung open, and narrowly missed Rollison's elbow. A man in the middle-twenties, wearing a black coat, striped trousers and a grey tie, and having the air of one who hadn't really had time to brush himself down that morning, came breezing in.

"Hallo, Mrs Regson," he said to the woman.

"Mr Hanbury!"

"Hanbury yesterday today and doubtless tomorrow," agreed the young man, good-humouredly. He looked too ruddy-faced, too bright-eyed and too eager to belong to such an ancient office as this.

"This gentleman says he has an appointment with you," declared Mrs Regson, as if resentfully.

Mr Hanbury looked surprised, stared at Rollison, rubbed his chin, and said:

"With me? Really?" Before Rollison could comment, he went on: "You sure it was with me?"

"It's Mr Rollison," said Mrs Regson.

"Eh? Oh, Mr *Rollison*! My dear sir. I'm so sorry. I expect you spoke to my uncle. He asked me to see you. I had to be in Court this morning. He knew I was coming in at eleven o'clock. Coffee?"

"Er——" began Rollison.

"Coffee for two, Mrs Regson," ordered young Mr Hanbury, and belatedly offered his hand. It was cool and firm. "Come in, come in."

He pushed a door open with his foot, and stood aside for Rollison to enter a long, narrow room, lined with books on one side and littered with black deed boxes and bundles of greying paper on the other. The one tall window was at the far end of the office from the door, and a desk was beneath it, with just room for a man to squeeze in between it and the wall. At this side of the desk stood a large arm-chair of creased and crumpled black leather. The desk itself was an unbelievable muddle of papers, on which, serving as a kind of mammoth paper-weight, was a hickory-shafted iron.

"Sit down, sit down, Mr Rollison," invited Mr Hanbury, and sat down himself, oblivious of the golf club. "I'm George Hanbury," he announced.

"Good morning," said Rollison, heavily.

"I'm afraid we are very short-handed. My secretary is away, and our managing clerk is ill. Mrs Regson is a retired secretary of the firm who lives upstairs, and she is always ready to help out." Thus Hanbury made it clear that the firm was very small. "Now to business! I have a feeling that I've heard your name before it cropped up in the will," said Hanbury. "*Richard* Rollison, isn't it?"

"Yes, Richard," answered Rollison.

"I'm very glad to meet you," said Mr Hanbury. "It was very good of you to come so quickly. Always like to get these matters settled as quickly as possible, you know. Probate's a funny thing. An estate can hang about for months if one doesn't know the ropes. Now, where is it?" He began to search among the papers on the desk with a preoccupied air. "I know it's here, I left it last night. I could have sworn I'd left it on top of—oh, half a mo'. I'll bet my uncle borrowed it." He jumped up, and made to stride past Rollison, but as if by accident Rollison shifted his position, and Mr Hanbury could not get past. "Excuse me," Hanbury said, brightly.

"Mr Hanbury."

"Yes, Mr Rollison?"

"Will you be good enough to tell me what this is all about?"

"I'm going to, I'm going to," promised Hanbury, warmly. "And I want you to understand one thing, Mr Rollison, the money is *clean*. The property is also *clean*. I have no time, no time at all, for any emotional or sentimental nonsense you might hear to the contrary. It's absolutely clean. Excuse me," added Mr Hanbury, and he skipped past Rollison with the agility of an Olympic hurdler at the top of his form, and disappeared through a doorway on the right. A moment later, Rollison heard him say clearly:

"I've got it."

2

THE LEGACY

GEORGE HANBURY came striding back in the same triumph, carrying a bundle of papers wrapped in red tape, and a large sheet of cardboard which looked rather like a photograph mount. Rollison reserved his opinion and exhorted himself to patience. Hanbury hopped over his legs again, slapped the bundle of papers on top of the golf club, and, in almost the same movement, thrust the sheet of cardboard in front of Rollison. It was indeed a photograph, with a sheet of tissue paper over it, and Rollison hesitated.

This had all the hall marks of a hoax, and he would not be too surprised if Hanbury had a distorted taste for the practical joke. He stood with the photograph thrust outwards, obviously longing for Rollison to flip the sheet of tissue aside, rather like a small child showing its father what he has bought him for a birthday present.

"There!" exclaimed Hanbury, and whisked the tissue away.

There was a photograph of a country house, an attractive Georgian country house, with lawns in front of flower beds at one side and in the distance some magnificent-looking trees.

"What do you think of *that*?" demanded Hanbury.

"I should say *circa* seventeen-fifty," said Rollison, "and probably in Hampshire or possibly Wiltshire."

"I *beg* your pardon. How can you possibly tell?"

"That scroll work over the door was a characteristic of Hampshire stonemasons about that time," declared Rollison. "It was used as a kind of signature."

"Indeed," said Hanbury, as if bewildered. "Well, well. I would never have known. You are quite right, of course.

The house is in Hampshire. I congratulate you, Mr
Rollison, I really do. A magnificent property."

"Yes, but——"

"With twenty-one acres and—believe it or not—with a
hundred and seven foot frontage on the river Agon, a
tributary of the Avon, one of the finest trout streams in the
south of England."

"That I believe," said Rollison. "But——"

"The fabric is in *perfect* condition," Hanbury went on
earnestly, "and I am assured that it will be remarkably
easy to maintain. The indoor staff, in fact, may be as few
as two persons. It will not be really expensive to put into
perfect condition, perfect, and——"

"Mr Hanbury."

"Yes, Mr Rollison."

"I am not in the market for a country house."

"Market?" echoed Hanbury. "I don't understand."

"At least we have something in common," said Rollison.
"What have I to do with this house?"

"But, my dear sir, you own it."

"I *what*?"

"But surely—oh, my goodness, I'm beginning to understand. My partner forgot to inform you about the legacy."
Hanbury was amazed, amused and appalled. "Why, how
positively absurd. I quite thought you knew. You must
think I'm bats. Well, well. Mr Rollison—you will be able
to establish your identity beyond any doubt, won't you?"

"Yes."

"Wonderful! Then this house is yours. Lock, stock,
barrel, garden and caretakers, if you require them. But if
you would prefer to employ a younger couple, provision
has been made in the will for Moody and his wife, the
present caretakers."

"Mr Hanbury," said Rollison, looking disbelievingly at
the photograph, "I know of no one who would leave me a
property like this."

"You don't?"

"No."

"You are Mr——" Hanbury sprang round to his desk, untied the red tape with a flick of his fingers, sorted out several sheets of parchment-like paper, and then looked challengingly at Rollison. "You are the Honourable Richard Rollison, D.S.O., M.C., Member of the Order of the British Empire, living at 22g, Gresham Terrace, Mayfair, London, West One."

"I am."

"Then there's no mistake. It is yours."

"Who left it to me?"

"I'm coming to that, Mr Rollison—are you quite comfortable? How about an ash tray? I—oh, here's the coffee." He sprang up. "Thank you, Mrs Regson." Two filled cups of black coffee were placed with unsteady hands near the handle of the golf club. The cups were of delicate pale blue china; the spoons were silver; the sugar bowl silver, too.

"Excuse me, sir," said the elderly woman.

"Yes?"

"May I be going up to my rooms, now? My boy is home today and he'll be wanting a midday meal."

"Of course, of course," said Hanbury. "Switch the telephone through to me." He waited until she had gone out, then explained as he handed Rollison the cream: "It's her grandson really. He's away a great deal, but he's her only relative, and she dotes on him. Ah. More cream, Mr Rollison?"

"A little, please."

"Good, good, good," clucked Hanbury, and sat back with his coffee balanced in one hand while he waved the other at Rollison. "You'll forgive me if I appear to patronise, Mr Rollison. I know you're an older man than I, but in these matters it is experience which counts, and I want you to understand that there is not the slightest need to have a moment's qualm, not a moment's qualm, about this inheritance. The ways of criminals are remarkable, in fact one might say incalculable. I know, I know indeed. I have had a great deal to do with them. Why, do you know, Mr Rollison, only last month, sitting in that very chair, the chair you are sitting in, there was a man who had *twice* been committed to prison for burglary! And consequently he was a hardened criminal. I know many others." The free hand waved comprehensively. "Many others. And believe it or not, they have their *good* side."

It was again beginning to occur to Rollison that he might be being taken for a ride; that George Hanbury knew perfectly well who he was, but had conceived of this as a droll practical joke. Rollison sat quite still, except for sipping coffee which was as good as any made by Jolly.

"Yes, these social misfits have their good side," went on Hanbury, sententiously. "Moreover, they are often very clever men. And although they may die and leave a large sum of money, that money isn't necessarily *tainted*. That is what I am so anxious to have you believe. It may have started in a somewhat unorthodox way, but many a criminal, having saved—to use a euphemism, Mr Rollison you understand me—having acquired, shall I say, a tidy little sum, will often invest it in stocks and shares and make a veritable fortune. And earlier of course he will have made restitution to society for any crimes, thefts or frauds. He will have served his prison sentence. I am going into this issue at some length because I fully understand that a man in your position, a man in society, a man unaccustomed to the crudities of crime, the seamy side of life shall I say, might be shocked by some of the revelations. But some of the most reputable of men undoubtedly garnered their first capital in somewhat dubious ways."

"Really," said Rollison, almost helplessly.

"Yes, indeed. And this man, your benefactor, paid the penalty for his crimes."

"Did he?"

"Yes, Mr Rollison, he did most certainly. He spent ten years in prison."

"I *see*."

"Mr Rollison, I want you to believe me when I say that ten years in prison can have a remarkable effect on a man. It can *reform* a man. I am quite sure that your benefactor was so reformed."

"Mr Hanbury——"

"And that his last ten years were lived in comfort of body, ease of spirit and freedom of conscience, Mr Rollison."

"No doubt," murmured Rollison. "Who was he?"

"Oh yes, of course, I'm coming to that. I don't want to give you any false impression. This man was old when he died, comparatively old, that is—he was seventy-one. He——"

"*Who was he?*"

Hanbury put his cup down firmly, squared his shoulders, and looked Rollison full in the eyes. He gave the impression that he had to steel himself to make the announcement, it would be so shocking; and Rollison wondered if it could possibly be an anti-climax after this great build-up.

"Your benefactor, Mr Rollison, is the late Mr Wilfrid Augustus Blacker. I have good reason to believe that he was more sinned against, in his early days, than sinning. He——"

"Gus *Blacker*?" exclaimed Rollison, astounded.

"You—you knew him well?"

Rollison said, with great and considered deliberation: "Are you seriously telling me that Gus Blacker bequeathed me that house? Gus *Blacker*?"

"He died a very wealthy man, Mr Rollison."

"That I can believe, but——"

"And I have no doubt that he realised that the upkeep of a house like Sandro Manor would tax the resources of any man, Mr Rollison. With the legacy there is a Trust Fund of fifty thousand pounds, yielding some three thousand pounds annually, *ample* to maintain the house and property. Of course, some capital expenditure will be

needed in the first place, but as the property is yours I have
no doubt that it will be possible to find a reasonable
mortgage, so that——"

"Did Blacker say anything in his will?"

"About what, Mr Rollison?"

"About why he left this to me?"

"Yes, indeed. He made a generous acknowledgement of
his debt to you."

"His debt?" echoed Rollison, faintly.

"Yes, Mr Rollison—and this simply bears out what I
have been saying, that very often a man with a criminal
record may have a heart of gold. One can never tell.
Here is a man who was convicted of—ah—murder, who
was considered fortunate to escape with his life, who
spent twenty-five of his first sixty years in prison, a man
whose reputation according to the one newspaper report
I have read was black, absolutely *black*. Nevertheless, he
felt so indebted to you for your help and guidance during
some of the periods in which he was not in prison——"

"Help and guidance!" Rollison almost choked.

"They are his very words, Mr Rollison. If you are not
convinced, read the actual will, which was prepared *by my
father* in this very office, three years ago. *Read*." Hanbury
scuffled over several thick sheets of the will, and then
thrust it, rather crumpled, in front of Rollison, indicating
a paragraph with his forefinger.

The paragraph, in jet black typewriting ink, said:

"And in token of his help and guidance during those
years when I was able to move freely about London, I
devise to the Hon. Richard Rollison of . . . my messuage
dwellinghouse and cottage and all outbuildings belong-
ing thereto known as Sandro Manor near Winchester
in the County of Hants and I give to him all my personal chattels therein. And in order that he may maintain the said dwellinghouse cottage and outbuildings in
a proper manner I GIVE to the Trustees of this will the

sum of £50,000 to invest the same in such investments as my Trustees shall in their absolute discretion think fit and to pay the income derived therefrom to the said Hon. Richard Rollison so long as he shall reside in and occupy the said dwellinghouse for a period of two calendar months in every year."

"You see," declared Hanbury, in triumph. "It could not be clearer."

"I do indeed see," murmured Rollison, huskily.

"I can well understand that you are overcome," said Hanbury. "It must be a great shock."

"Very great," agreed Rollison huskily. "Very great indeed." He took out his cigarette case and proffered it to Hanbury, who refused; he himself lit up, and watched the mushroom of grey smoke as it rose towards the ceiling. "Did you know Blacker at all?"

"No, indeed," said Hanbury. "My father knew him, though. He had great faith in my father."

"But you read about his trial—the last trial."

"Yes, yes," said Hanbury, as if he were a little annoyed. "But you really needn't take any notice of such dramatic outbursts, Mr Rollison. It is true that Mr Blacker swore from the dock that he would avenge himself upon the man who had sent him there, but these threats seldom come to anything, you know. In any case, consider the great stress under which Mr Blacker was living at the time. He had been convicted of murder. It was evident that the activities of one man—one individual—had enabled the police to complete their case. In fact, the police officer in charge of the investigations, a Superintendent Grice, stated publicly that without this private individual's assistance they would not have been able to win a conviction. You can surely understand the bitterness in Mr Blacker at the time, and the way in which that would express itself angrily, even venomously. Yet there is no reason to believe that this person who found the evidence against Mr

Blacker did in fact suffer. My father assured me that he did not, in any case. He had a somewhat peculiar name, I believe, a sobriquet. I always had a very bad memory for names, but this was very short, very pithy, so to speak. It was—now let me see."

"Could it have been the Toff?" inquired Rollison.

"Well, well, well! That is the very name, you have it in one—the *Toff*. I was surprised when I read through the newspaper report of the trial to find this—ah—Toff—referred to by his sobriquet. At the time, he must have been very well known. It didn't once give his real name, his surname. You don't happen to know that, also, do you?"

"You could try Rollison," said Rollison, and waited for the look of stupefaction to spread over young Mr Hanbury's face.

3

HELF FROM THE TOFF

It seemed a long time before Hanbury could find words;
a long time while his lips worked and his eyes appeared to
become larger and rounder, and his colour receded until
there was only pallor. Then, gradually, his expression
relaxed. He gulped. His large hands gripped the handle
of the golf club, as if he needed some kind of defensive
weapon. After all that, he contrived to ejaculate:

"No."

"Yes."

"You?"

"Me."

"No," breathed Hanbury.

"The facts are indisputable," declared Rollison.

"I can hardly believe it."

"I can understand your difficulty."

"No!" gasped Hanbury.

"Did you say a Trust which would yield three thousand
pounds a year?"

"You read it with your own eyes, Mr—Toff."

"I thought I read it."

"The house and grounds are worth——" Hanbury
choked.

"Twenty-five thousand pounds?"

"Fully twenty-five thousand pounds," agreed Hanbury.
"Well! How incredible. Remarkable."

"That's one way of saying it."

"What a perfect example."

"I beg your pardon?"

"What a perfect example of the sublime virtue of human
forgiveness."

"Oh."

"But you must see that," said Mr Hanbury, chokily. "This was the final act of redemption. Here was a man with a villainous record, a murderer, a hardened, ruthless criminal, who spent the last years of his life learning the great redeeming power of forgiveness. There is none greater. I am touched—I am deeply touched."

"I'm sure you are."

"But you must be much more deeply touched even than I."

"I must be," said Rollison. He stubbed out his cigarette, while Hanbury stared at the window, as if hoping to see the miracle of Gus Blacker's redemption written in large letters in the glass.

"Wonderful," breathed Hanbury.

"Mr Hanbury, when am I due to take over Sandro Manor?"

"You can take over within a very short time. I am sure that if you contemplate decorating the house and putting it in order, my firm, as Trustees, will be perfectly willing to allow you to start almost at once."

"When will the estate be cleared?"

"Well, you know, these large estates do take some time," said Hanbury, frowning. "Yes, indeed. Six months, perhaps—even a year. Certainly not less than four or five months, although I have known—let us say six months. But I do assure you, you can take possession whenever you wish."

"I think I'll wait," said Rollison. "I think I'll make sure that there isn't any mistake."

"My dear Mr Rollison," said George Hanbury earnestly, "I assure you that there isn't the slightest possibility of a mistake."

"Good."

"In fact there is only one other major beneficiary under the will, a Miss Lola Davenport who is at present in the United States of America. She was a close friend of Mr Blacker, I believe."

Rollison murmured: "How much does she get?"

"The residue of the estate, Mr Rollison, and while it is always unwise to guess, I imagine that the final figure will approximate five hundred thousand pounds. As no doubt you appreciate, that is quite a lot of money."

"Yes," said Rollison firmly. "I realise it very well. And what do I have to do next?"

"If you would be good enough to give me the name and address of your solicitors, and inform them that they will shortly be hearing from me, I will be grateful."

"I'll do that," said Rollison. "When will the news of the will be released?"

"I shall be registering it at Somerset House today," Hanbury told him, "and after that of course anyone who so desires may make an announcement. In view of the—ah—remarkable evidence of the change in Mr Blacker's attitude towards you, I imagine there will be quite a lot of publicity. A great deal. I do indeed. Will you find that embarrassing?"

"I hope not," said Rollison. "I certainly hope not."

A few minutes later Hanbury shook hands with him warmly, and saw him to the outer door. The young man had not fully recovered from his amazement at the remarkable change of heart in Gus Blacker. Rollison did not press the bell for the tiny lift. He looked at the sign pointing upwards, and reading *Caretaker*, then began to walk down the narrow wooden steps, slowly and thoughtfully; he needed time for reflection as he had seldom done before.

When he stepped out in Lincoln's Inn Fields, and looked across the parked cars and saw the people bustling to and from their legal chores, it seemed to him that wherever he went he could see the handsome face, the bushy eyebrows and the hard scowl of Gus Blacker. There had been a time, just before Blacker's arrest, when it had seemed likely that Jolly would soon be presiding discreetly over the funeral breakfast for his employer; the issue had been as close as that.

Rollison stepped into New Square, which was so very old. The sun had won the morning's battle; it was now nearly noon. He went on walking until he reached Piccadilly, oblivious of time. Near a hotel close by the Circus sat an old newspaper seller with three fingers missing from his left hand; fingers he had lost after a knife battle with Gus Blacker many years ago. The Toff went to him, and exchanged a halfcrown for an *Evening News*.

"Ta, Mr Ar. You keeping all right?"

"Pretty good, Simmy, on the whole."

"An ole pal of ours died a coupla days ago—you hear about that?"

"You mean Gus Blacker?"

"I mean Mr Flicking Blacker."

"Yes, I heard," said Rollison. "I was told that before he died, he reformed."

"He did *what*?" Simmy squeaked.

"He forgave everybody who had ever got in his way."

"No one's going to tell me that you fell for that mucky nonsense," said the newspaper seller. He had very small dark eyes set wide apart and he needed a shave; but his cloth choker and his cap were clean, and so were the fingers of his maimed hand. "He always said he would get you one day, Mr Ar. Never did, though. You've got the laugh on him now he's roasting."

"And what a laugh," said Rollison, and smiled and went down Piccadilly until he reached the turning which led first through Brook Street and then to Gresham Terrace. Everything was normal. He kept glancing over his shoulder, and was sure that somebody was following him; but there was no sign of anyone, no evidence at all.

Why should he be followed?

He was not involved in any case. It was at least four months since he had been, and for two of those months he had been in the South of France. Jolly had assured him that life had been uneventful during his absence. He had talked to Grice by telephone, and Grice had joked that there was no longer any need for the Toff; if the Yard could get along without him for two months, he could stay away as long as he liked.

The clear sky and the hot June sun seemed set fair, and so did Rollison's immediate future. Yet since he had heard of Gus Blacker's legacy he had felt as if he were living in shadows.

It was eerie, and it irritated him, because it was so clearly a matter of mood—and, although he hated to say so, a matter of nerves.

"Don't be a fool," he upbraided himself, and turned into the gateway of Number 22 Gresham Terrace. At the porch, he glanced right and left, to make sure that no one had followed him; except for two delivery vans and an old woman being dragged along by a large dog, the street was empty. He closed the door firmly, and then went upstairs, wondering how he would break this news to Jolly; it still had a quality of unreality. He reached the fifth and top floor, and was a little surprised, because Jolly had a remarkable habit of knowing when he was coming, and being at the door to greet him.

Rollison heard voices.

He turned his key in the lock gingerly, and opened the door an inch. Jolly would almost certainly know; a green light showed when the front door was opened with a key, part of the protection service which Jolly had developed because of the possibility of reprisals from such men as Gus Blacker—when unreformed.

A woman was speaking in a pleasant American accent, not harsh or strident, but most definitely American.

". . . and I was so excited I had to come right here. I just had to see Mr Rollison before I went to see anybody else. I wouldn't feel safe in England without some kind of expert protection. Mr Jolly, will you do me one very great favour?"

"If it is in my power," Jolly said, in a constricted voice.

"That's very sweet of you." There was a pause, the

kind of pause which might come between lovers if there was an interruption for a kiss or a squeeze or a hug; but it was less the pause than the tone of Jolly's voice which affected Rollison. That "If it is in my power", could have been meant ironically or sarcastically, but Jolly had been not only earnest but almost emotional. In such circumstances, that was almost incredible.

"That's very, very sweet of you," repeated the American visitor. "Mr Jolly, what I want you to promise is just this: you will do everything in your power to persuade Mr Rollison to help me?"

"I am quite sure that he will need no persuasion," said Jolly, and again it was obvious that he meant precisely what he said.

"I most certainly hope you are right," said the visitor. There was another pause, and a little squeaking sound, as if of delight. Not a *kiss*? "Now Mr Jolly, honey, I want you to tell me all about this remarkable collection of weapons. I guess I should call them all lethal weapons. Now don't tell me, I know what you call it, just let me think and it'll come back."

Rollison stepped inside the lounge hall, closed the door softly, and went towards the large living-room-cum-study where Jolly and the woman were. The door was half open.

Rollison was able to see inside, but at first that did not greatly help him. Jolly and the visitor had their backs to him. They were between his desk and his Trophy Wall. The girl was looking up at it, one hand raised a little higher than her head. She was several inches taller than Jolly, and all that Rollison could see from the back was that she was dark-haired and had a slender figure and quite beautiful legs.

Jolly stood absolutely still and silent.

"No, don't tell me, I'm sure I can remember," said the American, and suddenly she turned towards Jolly, gripped his arms just above the wrists, and cried: "It's called the Trophy Wall!"

"That is exactly right," said Jolly.

Now Rollison could see the girl in profile, and he could understand a great deal. It wasn't so much her figure, although that had to be seen to be believed. It was her face. She had that rare kind of peach-blossom complexion in which it was hard to believe, and quite indescribably beautiful features. In fact, Rollison found it difficult to realise that she was real. Yet there she stood smiling at Jolly as if at a fond parent, holding Jolly's hands, giving the impression that at any moment she would draw him close and squeeze him against that magnificent bosom. Jolly, to do him justice, was obviously feeling embarrassed, yet under her spell.

"So my memory didn't fail me, Mr Jolly."

"No, that is Mr Rollison's Trophy Wall," murmured Jolly.

Rollison moved back, out of sight, so that he would not be seen accidentally. He was half smiling, half frowning. He went back to the outer door, and hesitated with his hand on it. The visitor began to ask Jolly what this, that and the other was, and he waited until she wanted to know about "this cute little dagger, did that kill anyone?" before he opened the door, and then closed it loudly. He did not hear Jolly exclaim, but heard the girl say:

"Why, what's the matter?"

"If you will excuse me——" began Jolly.

"Is that Mr Rollison in person?" cried the girl, and Rollison heard a flurry of footsteps and Jolly's almost inarticulate effort to stop her. The door opened wide and the girl came into sight. Full-face, she was as devastating as in profile. Unwarned, Rollison would have been astounded, for she was the kind to turn any man to a gaping goon. As it was, he still could not really believe in her.

Just behind her, came Jolly.

"Mr Rollison," he began, as if he had a frog in his throat, "this is Miss——"

"Mr Rollison, I want to tell you how perfectly charming Mr Jolly has been to me while you've been out. He's been the perfect English gentleman, and I want you to know that I appreciate it very much indeed." She moved as she spoke, with a curiously swaying action. Every step was considered; so, he was sure, was every movement of her eyes, every hint of a smile. She slowed down as she drew near, and held out both hands. "Mr Rollison, I'm Lola Davenport, and I just had to come and see you. I really do need your help."

4

LOLA

THERE were two ways to react.

Rollison could submit to this palpitating beauty, and be submerged by her overwhelming personality; or he could take the wind right out of her sails. Perhaps because he was still affected by the shadow of Gus Blacker, and because she was the heiress of nearly half a million of Gus's ill-gotten gains, he had a momentary qualm. Lola was so near him that in a moment their hands would touch, and she would do as she had with Jolly, squeeze his hands and beam upon him rather like a favourite Aunt greeting a long absent child.

Her eyes had a mesmeric kind of effect; they held a glowing radiance which could hypnotise any man. And she was so absolutely sure of herself.

"Why, Lola," murmured Rollison, and decided that it must be her turn to be at disadvantage.

He moved his hands swiftly, slid his right arm round her waist and his left round her shoulders, and drew her to him in a bear hug that sent the wind rushing out of her lungs. He felt her brassière'd fullness against his chest, placed his cheek against hers, and held her tight and tighter. He could feel her breathing hard, then gasping for breath; but she did not struggle and made no attempt to free herself. It was as if she knew that the only way to gain the ascendancy was to make him let her go.

Her ear was very close to his lips.

"Lola," he whispered, "how wonderful to see you."

She made no attempt to speak, and did not move; but now her breath was coming in shorter gasps, and he could hear her heart palpitating. Behind her, Jolly moved, turning away as if he could not bear the sight.

Lola Davenport began to writhe in Rollison's arms, and soon to lose a little of her colour; he let her go. At first, she swayed, but as Rollison did not help her she put out her hand to steady herself. This time she made no attempt to take hold of him; the radiance had faded from her eyes and she looked as if she would fall if she could not keep hold on him. Gradually she steadied.

There were tinkling noises, and Rollison saw that Jolly had so far recovered his *sang-froid* that he had taken out whisky, gin and assorted drinks, and put them on a tray, with several glasses. As he carried these to the desk, he seemed to be making a special effort to keep both steady and poised. His face, lined and slightly baggy beneath the eyes, and even baggier beneath the chin, had lost its customary look—of the dyspeptic.

He said: "Will that be all, sir?"

"All for now, Jolly," Rollison said.

"Very good, sir." Jolly turned and walked to the door leading to the domestic quarters of the flat, rather like a man in a daze.

Lola was now just touching the top of Rollison's shoulder with her fingers, and standing at arm's length.

"And what will you have to drink?" he inquired.

She began: "I'd just love——" in a husky voice, broke off, took her hand away, and stared at him. Then she made a second attempt. "I would just love a dry Martini."

"Then that's what we'll have. Jolly! Some ice—oh, there is ice. Won't you sit down?" Rollison took Lola Davenport's arm firmly and led her to a small armchair which had a fairly straight back; a chair in which she could sit with comfort but without falling back. She was very glad of his help to sit. He turned his back on her, put ice into a blue-tinted glass jug, poured in gin, shook and rattled the mixture with the restrained vigour of an expert bar-tender; and he took much longer than necessary over it, because now he wanted Lola to have time to recover. There were limits to the advantage that he could take even of the Lolas of this world.

At last he turned round, glasses in hand.

She was sitting back, poised. Her legs were crossed, and her rounded knees showed. Those legs were as slender and as attractive when she was sitting as when she had been standing, and the adjustment of the skirt was beautifully judged allure. She wore a linen suit, with huge yellow flowers against a green background, most modest at the neck; and she had adjusted the collar and touched up her hair while Rollison's back had been turned.

He handed her the drink.

"To happy days in London," he toasted.

"Happy days," she echoed. Now it was obvious that she had recovered her breath completely, but she was looking at him warily. Her drink vanished. Rollison sipped his, and went back for the jug. "Another?"

"Why, thank you."

He poured out carefully. Her hands were pristine pale, and the pink-tinted nails shapely and lovely; her appearance was almost impossible to fault.

"When did you arrive in England?" Rollison inquired.

"Just this morning."

"As recently as that? You must let me show you round London."

"I'd love you to."

"It can be quite a place," said Rollison. "What made you come to see me?"

She sipped her drink, looked up at him, and obviously felt at some disadvantage because she was sitting down. He lowered himself to the arm of a chair.

"I just had to," she said. "I was in such need of help."

"What made you think I could help you?"

"Why, Mr Rollison, your reputation. What else would? Don't tell me that you don't realise that you're as famous in the United States as you are in your home country. Why, you're known to be the most remarkable private eye since Sherlock Holmes!"

Rollison laughed. "Not in England, and certainly not in the United States. They call me a lot of things but never Holmes. Someone told you that I sometimes play detective, did they?"

"*Played* detective? Why, they told me——"

"Lola," interrupted Rollison, "skip the blarney."

His eyes were laughing at her, and he wondered if he could win a responding laugh. If she had a sense of humour, then she was not far off the perfect woman; and if she had any sense of humour at all, it would reveal itself now. She stared at him for what seemed a long time, as if she did not quite understand what he was getting at. Then her incredibly perfect lips began to curve at the corners, a shadow of a dimple appeared on either cheek, her eyes began to crinkle at the corners, too. Suddenly, she began to laugh, and Rollison found the laugh so infectious that he joined in. Glancing towards the door, he saw Jolly hovering; Jolly was giving the most expansive smile.

"Mr Rollison," Lola said at last, "I'm very glad I met you. We're going to have ourselves quite a time, I can see that."

"Quite a time," agreed Rollison warmly. "Ready for another?"

"No, sir, I'm not going to drink any more while you're around. I'll need all my wits about me."

"I'm a very simple person," Rollison declared.

"Oh, sure, you're simple. You're very simple. You're very direct in what you do, I'll just have to admit that. Now you want to know why I came straight to you from the airport? All I did was to check in at my hotel and come straight here."

"What hotel?"

"The Rolchester."

"You ought to move to the Connaught."

"Tell me why."

"It's round the corner from here."

She laughed again.

"I'll change hotels just as soon as I can, if you'll undertake to look after me."

"I'll undertake to try, but—why do you need looking after?"

She said: "You have to believe me, Mr Rollison." She put her glass down on a table by the side of her chair, uncrossed her legs and kept them very close together, slanting them a little to one side. All vestige of a smile disappeared. She had obviously set herself to convince him beyond all possible doubt. "Before I left New York, two attempts were made on my life."

"Really?"

"I told you that you just have to believe me."

"Convince me," invited Rollison.

She said: "You must take my word for it, Mr Rollison. I was walking from my apartment to a taxi, just across the street. The doorman had taken my baggage across. I just had to cross the street. And if the doorman hadn't shouted to warn me, a car would have run me down."

Rollison said: "Where was this?"

"On 61st Street near Fifth Avenue."

"And the second attempt?"

"The same kind of attack," said Lola Davenport earnestly, "but at the airport this time. There was a long line of cars and taxis waiting, and I was always an impatient person, so I got out of my taxi to walk. A car like the one which had nearly run over me on 61st Street was in the other lane, and the driver tried to run me down, also. I tried to see him, but I only saw the top of his head."

"Did you know the car?"

"It was a blue Chevrolet, I am positive of that."

"How did he come to miss you the second time?"

She looked at Rollison as if reproachfully, then quite deliberately but very quickly she stretched out her left leg and slid her hand beneath her skirt. There was a quick flurry of movement of those long, lovely fingers, and suspenders slipped open. She rolled down her left stocking with the expert ease which always fascinates a man, and showed that on her leg from the knee down there was no blemish, but a few inches above the knee was an ugly looking graze.

"He missed because I jumped out of the way, and I ran into a baggage truck. This is the result of the collision."

"Ah," said Rollison. "Have you had any treatment for that?"

"I have not, but——"

"You ought to have it bathed, and a lotion put on," Rollison said earnestly. "Jolly is a very good first aid man." When she didn't answer, simply pulled up her stocking and smoothed down her skirt, he went on: "Does it hurt?"

"It hurts when I touch it or knock against something."

"Jolly will fix it," said Rollison, and pressed a bell. Jolly appeared as if by magic. "Jolly, Miss Davenport has a nasty bruise and graze on her left leg—will you get a lotion ready in the bathroom?"

"At once, sir."

"Let me know when it's ready," said Rollison, quite aware that Lola was watching him not only warily but suspiciously. "So there were two attempts to run you down, but they didn't prevent you from coming to London."

"They certainly did not. It seemed to me that New York was a good place to get away from."

"Do you know why you were attacked?"

Lola said: "Mr Rollison, do you believe me or don't you?"

"Of course I believe you."

"This really happened, you know."

"I've seen the bruise."

"I could have——" she began, and then gave up,

leaned forward, and went on: "No, sir, I can't imagine why anyone should attempt to kill me. I don't lead an exciting life."

Rollison murmured: "That I can't believe!"

She laughed. "I mean your kind of exciting life, I guess. I am a night-club singer, Mr Rollison, and nobody seems to care that I can't sing very well."

"That I can understand," Rollison said.

"You just have to, because it's true also. I have a number of admirers whose wives don't exactly approve of me, but I can't help it if a man wants to buy me a drink, or send me a bouquet. I don't know of a single person in New York with a reason for wanting to kill me. I only know that some guy tried to, twice."

"Would you recognise him again?"

"I most certainly would not."

"Did you report these attempts to the police?"

"The police at Idlewild called the driver crazy, and said they would book him."

"Did they?"

"I don't believe they caught up with him."

"We'll find out," Rollison said, and moved across to his desk, to the visitor's obvious surprise. He lifted the telephone and dialled a number; she was not to know that it was the number of a national newspaper. "Is Mr Clayton there?" inquired Rollison, and a moment later he went on: "Clayt, will you try to find out for me if the police at Idlewild Airport, New York, picked up a man for dangerous driving at the airport yesterday—what time was your airplane, Miss Davenport?"

"It left Idlewild at nine-thirty."

"The incident happened about nine-thirty, Eastern Standard Time," Rollison went on. "Will you fix it?" He held on for a moment, then said "Thanks," and rang off.

As he did so, Jolly appeared in the doorway again. "Everything ready, Jolly?" Rollison asked, in the same breath.

"Yes, sir."

"Would you like to fix this yourself, or will you talk to me while Jolly acts as nurse?" inquired Rollison.

Lola laughed again. "So long as you're both there."

"Come along, then," said Rollison, and led the way through the doorway, along the passages with doors on either side, and then into a small, beautifully appointed modern bathroom. Jolly had ready two bowls of water, antiseptic, gauzes and plaster; everything that could be needed. "Sit on the stool and put your leg up on the side of the bath," ordered Rollison, and as Lola did so, Jolly took a thick towel and folded it under her leg, so that there would be no hardness from the bath itself. "Now!" went on Rollison, briskly. "You got on the aircraft. Had you decided to come and see me by that time?"

"Yes, I had, but I would not have come so soon but for the attacks."

"Why come to see me?"

"Well, I guess you know that we are the two people who inherit Gus Blacker's money," she said, "so we had that in common, at least. I'll tell you the truth, Mr Rollison. When I heard about that will and about you I asked a friend on the *New York Times* for information, and he told me everything he knew about you. It was plenty! And I didn't like the idea of being squashed by an auto, either. This newspaperman told me that there wasn't a man in England better at his job than you, so naturally, I came straight to you."

"Via the Rolchester."

"Yes."

"Were you followed from the hotel?"

"Not as far as I know," Lola answered, and twisted round to look at him more squarely. What that did to the top half of her body made Jolly momentarily close his eyes. "Why, Mr Rollison, would you expect me to be followed?"

"I just wanted to know," said Rollison.

"If you mean, did anyone attack me, then the answer is

no. The journey from London Airport was quite uneventful. I was very much relieved when I reached here safely. But I have to admit that I don't know whether those attacks on me were caused by something I'd done in New York without realising it, or whether they had anything to do with Gus Blacker's will. Gus's lawyers telephoned me about that. He made me a rich woman, Mr Rollison—a million and a half dollars is a lot of money."

Rollison said: "Yes, isn't it? And who would get it if you didn't?"

"You mean, if I were to die?"

"That's exactly what I mean."

"I don't know who would get it," said Lola. "That's what I want you to find out."

5

NEXT BENEFICIARY

"Excuse me, Miss," said Jolly, apologetically.

"Yes, Mr Jolly?"

"I could put a dressing on your leg, if you so desire, but I think you will find it quite comfortable as it is, provided you don't wear anything harsh or rough against the skin."

Lola looked at his balding head, and gave a ridiculous impression that she was tempted to kiss it.

"I don't make a habit of wearing anything harsh against any of my skin, Jolly."

"If I may say so, Miss, nylon can be quite harsh."

"What's that?"

"I said nylon——"

"Jolly," she interrupted, "those panties are *pura seta*."

"Then there should be no excessive irritation of the bruise," said Jolly, solemn-faced. "An ordinary brand of zinc cream or ointment, applied at night, should be all that is required from now on. Excuse me, sir."

"Yes?" said Rollison.

"Will you be in for lunch?"

Rollison looked at Lola. "Shall we be in?"

"Are you inviting me to have lunch with you?"

"Yes. Here, or at a restaurant."

"I think I would love to have lunch here," declared Lola. "You may not believe it, but I didn't get much sleep on that aircraft, and I would be very happy not to have to go out again for a while."

"We'll be in for lunch," Rollison said to Jolly, and his man departed, doubtless to perform miracles in the kitchen.

Rollison took Lola back to the big room, poured her out

another drink, and watched as she sipped it as if determined not to allow herself to drink too much.

"Will you find out who would get that money if I were to die?" asked Lola.

"It shouldn't be difficult," said Rollison. He went to the telephone again; and, as he stretched out his hand to touch it, the bell rang. He picked up the receiver, said: "Speaking," waited for a moment, then went on: "Hallo, Clayt . . . Very quick work, thanks . . . He *did*? . . . That's all I need right now, but ask your New York correspondent if he will follow it up, will you? . . . Yes, there'll be a story, sooner or later . . . I . . . *What*?" His voice changed slightly and he stared at the Trophy Wall, as if intrigued by a hangman's rope which hung with ominous menace from a swivel. "I see," he went on, heavily. "Very interesting. If I see her, I'll tell you." He rang off, very slowly, and contemplated Lola, who sat back in the chair and seemed to challenge him to comment. "Lola, honey," he murmured.

"May I call you Richard?"

"You may call me Richard or Rolly or whatever you like. It's what you tell me that matters."

"I don't understand you."

"There are at least three wives who would like to cut your throat," Rollison murmured. "You have the hottest reputation of any night club queen in the whole of the United States, and when the New York correspondent of the *London Globe* heard that you had been involved in this incident he just cried *Wow!* And he warned everyone involved to make sure they didn't get burnt."

"He's exaggerating," Lola declared.

"Would a jealous wife hire a driver to run you down?"

"I can't imagine anyone being so crazy."

"They might be satisfied with spoiling your looks."

Lola stared; then gave a little shudder.

"I do wish you hadn't said that. I'm very sensitive about my features."

"I want you to understand how dangerous the situation could be."

"You don't have to tell me."

"Is there anything else you've kept back from me?"

"No, Richard," Lola said. She made the 'ch' sound soft, so that the name was a cross between Ri*ch*ard and Ri*sh*ard. "And I don't believe these wives would be so jealous as all that."

"It depends what you did to their husbands," Rollison said dryly.

He picked up the telephone again, and dialled the number of Gammon and Hanbury's Lincoln's Inn office, watched the American woman as he did so, and heard the dialling sound. The unmistakable voice of the elderly Mrs Regson came on the line.

"Yes, sir, Mr Hanbury is in," she said, without a trace of vagueness, and a moment later Hanbury came on brightly. "George Hanbury speaking."

"This is Richard Rollison——"

"Mr Rollison!" exclaimed Hanbury, and gave the impression of being even more self-assured than he had been when Rollison had left him. "I'm very glad you called, sir. I want you to know that I understand what a complete ass I made of myself this morning. It has taught me a big lesson, you can be sure of that."

"Forget it," said Rollison. "Just tell me who will inherit Blacker's money, the big money, if Miss Lola Davenport were to die."

"If she were to *what*?"

"Die."

"*I don't know that I like this kind of conversation*," Lola said into Rollison's ear; she had moved very close to him.

"But surely you have no reason to suspect——" Hanbury began, shrilly.

"I've heard that she has had a very grave illness lately."

"Good gracious me!"

"Who would?"

"Who would what?"

"Mr Hanbury——"

"I'm sorry, I'm sorry," broke in Hanbury hastily. "You gave me quite a shock, you know. Well, the answer is very simple, Mr Rollison. No one would inherit that money direct from the estate. Miss Davenport is the beneficiary. Since she outlived Mr Blacker, on her death any money due to her under the terms of Mr Blacker's will goes to her next of kin, or to any person or persons named in her will. Apart from your good self, the Moodys at Sandro Manor, and a few very small bequests for old times' sake, there are no other legacies."

"Thank you," said Rollison.

"I do hope that—but Mr Rollison!"

"Yes."

"I had a cable only this morning, saying that Miss Davenport is on her way to London. I talked to her by telephone yesterday, and she sounded in the best of health."

"Oh, she's in the best of health," confirmed Rollison. "At the moment. Thanks, Mr Hanbury." He rang off, put his head on one side, and studied Lola. He realised with relief that he was at last becoming inured to that mesmeric beauty; but that the word "ravishing" was the only one which was really apt.

Now she was worried, and consequently a little solemn. She moved further away from him, towards the Trophy Wall, and seemed oblivious of the fact that her head was within a few inches of the hangman's rope.

"Who would get the dough?" she inquired.

"Your next of kin, or anyone you named in your will." She said softly: "Is that so?"

"Who is your next of kin?" Rollison demanded.

"I don't want to talk about that," said Lola. "Not right now, anyway. No one could have tried to kill me because of the inheritance."

"Why not?"

"I didn't tell anybody about it."

Rollison asked, as if astonished: "No one at all?"

"No one."

"You mean to tell me that you heard that you had inherited over a million dollars and didn't confide in a single person?"

"I did not."

"Why not?"

"Mr Rollison," said Lola, very formally, "you don't go around telling the girls in the strip chorus or the bartender or the hostess or even the club manager that you are going to inherit a million bucks. You just don't do that if your head is where it ought to be. For one reason they will start by thinking you're nuts. Then if they start to believe you, suddenly they think up ways of helping themselves to the money."

"No friends?" inquired Rollison.

She was very emphatic. "No friends as good as that."

"Relations?"

"No relations I know of."

"So no one in New York knows about this inheritance as far as you know."

"Who would tell them if I didn't?"

Rollison said: "That is one of the things we have to find out. But if no one you've robbed of a husband tried to kill you, and no husband who thinks you might squeeze him for his past sins, then who wanted you dead?"

After a long pause, she said: "Richard, if I live I'm going to be a very rich woman."

"So?"

"If I inherited a million dollars, that would be a million. If I inherited a million and a half, it wouldn't make much difference to me. Everything over the first million I could afford to give away. That's a pile of money."

"Well?"

"You can earn a big share of it by finding out the

answers to all these questions, and by making sure that I live to spend my million dollars. Will you do that?"

Rollison said: "I think I would have a go, but you'll have to fix all the financial side of it with Jolly."

"Don't tell me you're too proud to handle money!"

Rollison laughed. "I'm just too sentimental, and Jolly doesn't approve of me working for nothing. Lola——"

He paused, and studied her. She didn't look away. He thought that she was as frightened as she made out to be, and he wondered what she had not told him. He doubted whether this was a moment to try to make her confide further; sooner or later she would tell him all he needed to know.

"Yes?" she said.

"You're not going to the Connaught Hotel."

"Just as you say."

"You're staying here."

"If you say so."

"I say so until we're sure that there's no danger."

"Do you have any idea how long that will be?"

"No," said Rollison, "but I do know that over the years this apartment has been attacked from all sides, above and below. One of the first men to break in was Gus Blacker. He planned to crush my skull with a plumber's hammer."

Lola didn't respond.

"And while nothing can be guaranteed, I can send for some friends from the East End of London, so that the place is never left unprotected, whether we're in or out. That wouldn't be so easy at a hotel."

"I can see that," Lola said. "But I unpacked one of my bags, I needed to put on a different suit. Can I go back to the Rolchester and pack that bag again?"

"We'll go together," said Rollison. "Lola."

"Yes?"

"Have you any friends or acquaintances in England?"

"No, I have not."

"Do you know any English people?"

"I guess I've met some English business men in New York, but when business men are tired for the evening it's difficult to tell the difference between the American and the English or the Eskimo."

"Is there any one at all in England who might want to harm you—apart from anyone who might hate you for getting Blacker's money?"

"I don't believe so."

"How well did you know Blacker?"

Lola said: "I wondered when you would get around to asking that, Richard. I didn't know Gus real well, but I was a good friend to him when he first came over to New York, five years ago."

"Was that his only visit?"

"No, sir. He came each year afterwards."

"To see you?"

"He seemed to think that was a good enough reason."

"How long did he stay?"

"Usually around two months," answered Lola. "He would follow wherever I was appearing, and would come to see me at Vegas, or Miami, or Hollywood or New York —any place I was on show. He liked to get around."

"With you?"

"Yes, sir, with me."

"How did you get to know him?"

"We just got acquainted, I guess. That isn't difficult in my profession."

"You have to get very well acquainted to inherit one and a half million dollars."

"We were *very* well acquainted."

"Did you know he had served a prison sentence for murder?"

"I knew he'd been in trouble and was in New York on a false passport because of his past," answered Lola. "But he didn't go into any details. He wasn't married, or anything like that, and didn't have a jealous wife."

"No," said Rollison, thoughtfully. "He didn't get

married as far as we know. He always worked alone, too —except when he bribed or terrorised other men to do what he wanted. Gus was a lone wolf, and I don't know of anyone who would think he or she had a good right to his fortune. Lola."

"Yes?"

"Are you his daughter?" Rollison inquired.

6

DAUGHTER?

LOLA DAVENPORT looked very hard and intently at Rollison, as if she did not know how to answer that question. Rollison moved slowly away from the chair towards the Trophy Wall, and was very close to a small, heavy-headed hammer. A motor-cycle scorched along outside, and a long way off a radio was playing; otherwise there were no sounds.

"Richard," Lola said at last, "why did you ask that question?"

"I'd like to know the answer."

"That isn't what I mean."

"Gus was a tall man," Rollison said, "and he was very handsome—one of the most handsome men I ever knew. He had no difficulty in getting any woman he wanted—married or unmarried, young and simple or middle-aged and sophisticated. I should say that Gus Blacker wrecked more marriages than any man before or since, but I must say one thing for him."

Lola said, tight-lipped: "That will be quite a concession. You didn't like him at all, did you?"

"I didn't like him at all," agreed Rollison. He took the hammer off its hook, to which it was attached by a narrow leather strap. He weighed it in the air, thoughtfully, and Lola looked at it as if hypnotised. "But he was fastidious where women were concerned. He was a connoisseur of feminine beauty, and nothing but the best interested him. If Blacker had a child it would be by a beautiful woman, and there's a good chance that the child would be as lovely as you."

Lola did not seem to hear him.

"So, I'd like to know," said Rollison.

46

She drew a deep breath. "So would I," she said.

"Lola."

"Yes?"

"He was a cruel, sadistic devil and one of the worst men I've ever met, but he wasn't a pervert. Did he share your apartment with you?"

"No," she replied quickly. "Nor my bed."

"Did you refuse that?"

"He always made a joke of being an old man, saying he took only a grandfather's interest in me."

"Did you ever suspect that he was your father?"

"It passed through my mind."

"So you didn't know your father?"

"Or my mother," Lola answered. "I didn't have it very good when I was young, Richard. My birth certificate gave my mother's name as O'Ryan and my father as unknown—at times, like when I fill out forms for a passport, that can be embarrassing."

"I can imagine," Rollison said. Then he espied Jolly hovering, knew that luncheon was ready, and was quite sure that it would be a meal fit for a gourmet.

Obviously Lola enjoyed it. She was lavish with her praise, and yet her heart wasn't in anything that she did or said—if Rollison was right. It became increasingly obvious that she was very tired; within ten minutes of drinking coffee, her eyes looked heavy enough to close of their own accord. Rollison took her into the guest room, and left the key on the inside.

"That bed looks so good I doubt if I'll get up again today," she said, and for the first time since luncheon and the question about her "father" she looked as if she was really herself again.

She was sound asleep when Rollison went in and opened her handbag, took out her keys, and a slip which told him that her room at the hotel was 517.

* * *

"Jolly," said Rollison, "we must be very careful."

"That is most evident, sir."

"Tell Ebbutt that we need a day and night guard, six men all the time. Percy Wrightson and his wife had better come and live in, and Mrs Wrightson can do some of the chores."

"That will be very welcome, sir."

"I'm going over to the Rolchester to get Miss Davenport's baggage. It shouldn't take more than an hour. If she's still asleep when I get back, I think I'll go round and see Grice. See if he can make an appointment for half past four, will you?"

"I will," promised Jolly.

"Thanks," said Rollison, and turned away. Then suddenly he swung round. "But you don't know, do you?"

Jolly looked puzzled.

"About what, sir?"

"The house—the house called Sandro Manor."

"I don't think the name is familiar."

"It will be," Rollison said, heavily. "If I like to be fool enough to take it, it's mine. Gus Blacker left it to me, and three thousand a year to keep it up."

Jolly said, astounded: "*Blacker* did?"

"Yes."

"Then we need to be very careful indeed, sir—extremely careful, especially of anything at the house. There can be no doubt at all that he never forgave you, and——"

Jolly broke off, as if overcome by the news.

"He'd have got a kick out of laying on his revenge after his death," mused Rollison. "Yes, I know he would have. There's a curious likeness between him and Miss Davenport, too. Have you seen it?"

"A facial likeness?" inquired Jolly.

"Something much more subtle."

Jolly said, very slowly and almost painfully: "I think perhaps I know what you mean, sir. Blacker had an absolutely irresistible way with the opposite sex. It was almost impossible for them to resist him once he made up his mind to a conquest. Anyone observing them dispassionately would be astonished at how obvious his methods were, but they always succeeded. Is that what you mean?"

"Go on."

"Miss Davenport has that same kind of—of personal magnetism, sir. That is quite evident."

"Yes," agreed Rollison. "That's it. Better warn Percy Wrightson about it."

"I shall indeed," said Jolly. "Er—there is one other relevant matter."

"What's that?"

"I heard a little of the conversation you had with Miss Davenport," Jolly said, straight-faced, "and heard your question about the possibility that Blacker was her father." When Rollison made no comment, Jolly went on: "It is quite possible that he was, that she is aware of it, and that he arranged for her to—ah—work on you. You will recall that you finally caught Blacker through a woman whom he had betrayed and who was bitterly resentful and vengeful. Nothing would give him greater satisfaction than to make you—ah—enamoured of a woman, and then to ruin you because of the association. It is the kind of Machiavellian trick which——"

"Jolly."

"Sir?"

"Blacker is dead."

"So I understand, sir."

"But you talk of him as if he were alive and getting ready to laugh his head off."

"I know exactly what you mean," said Jolly.

Rollison also knew exactly what he meant as he walked from Gresham Terrace to Piccadilly. He was not followed, and yet had a sense of being watched all the time. He made several detours, to make sure that no one showed any interest in him and no one did.

At last he got a taxi and sat back in a corner, watching behind him all the time. When he paid the taxi off, and the massive uniformed doorman at the Rolchester pushed the hotel door open for him, a man stepped from one side, and Rollison actually caught his breath. It was absurd.

He went to the desk and asked for the key to Room 517; a youthful porter handed it to him. Before going to the lift, Rollison studied the dozen or so men in the foyer, and the little group of sleek and fashionable women sitting round a table and having tea.

A coloured youth took him up to the fifth floor. No one was at the landing. He passed a teen-age maid at a telephone in a cubicle marked *Service Only* and gathered from the way she stopped talking that the conversation wasn't strictly business. He reached a corner and saw an arrow pointing to Rooms 511 to 529. A long window at the end of the passage reminded him of Hanbury's office, and told him that each of the rooms had a view of Hyde Park. It was very quiet up here. He put the key in the lock of Room 517, and twisted it slowly and without a sound; when the lock turned, he pushed the door open an inch.

He heard nothing.

He pushed the door wide enough to get through, then withdrew into the passage and kicked the door open vigorously; it banged against the wall and swung back sluggishly towards him. Only then did he go inside.

There was a small drawing-room, and a door leading to the bedroom, with the bathroom leading off a shallow, tiled passage. He locked and bolted the door, then checked that the bathroom and bedroom were empty, and satisfied himself that no one lurked on this balcony or on the balconies within reach.

He went back into the apartment.

A pair of gossamer-thin nylon stockings were draped over the end of the brass-panelled bedstead, a few make-up oddments were dotted about the dressing table, some cotton wool with lipstick or rouge on it was on the trinket tray. A sprinkling of powder lay upon the glass of the dressing-table top. Two suitcases, one on top of the other, were on the luggage stool, the top one with its clasps up, the bottom one secured.

He went to the stockings, picked them up, ran them through his fingers, and saw that each was laddered, one of them very badly. As far as he could judge the damage had started fairly high, near the double-thickness patch for suspender fastening. The other started about the knee. He put these down, and went to the wardrobe, opening it very cautiously. Another cotton suit, of flecked green and red, hung inside. He took this down and examined the skirt; there was a small tear at about the spot where Lola said she had banged against the baggage truck.

Rollison turned towards the cases.

He stood and examined them for some seconds, looking for fresh scratches. There seemed to be none on the top, but he took out a small magnifying glass and studied the metal plate of the fastening; there were fairly fresh scratches. He examined the lower case; there, the scratches were much brighter, as if someone had tried to force the locks.

"It's just possible," Rollison said, *sotto voce*. He turned to the bed, picked up a pillow, went back to the cases and, holding the pillow in front of his face, prised up the lid of the top one. Nothing happened. When he had it right up, he put the pillow on one side, scoffing at himself.

The clothes inside were all expensive, fragile and, as far as he could judge, very well looked after. The packing was very tidy too; nothing was out of place. He lifted the top things out; two brassières, some panties, a folded slip, stockings, handkerchiefs, a clothes brush—and found nothing he would not expect. He lifted this case down, took out Lola's keys and unlocked both clasps.

Then he picked up the pillow again and repeated his manoeuvre with the first case. As the lid came up, he felt his smile becoming tense. He raised it very slowly, and his breathing was becoming quicker; more like Lola's when he had pressed her against him.

The lid was half-way up when he felt it stop. He did not push harder, just held it in position, then held the pillow away and peered inside the half-open case. Two straps appeared to be stuck, one on each side, at the point of the joint of the hinge and the lid. He stepped to one side, still holding the lid, covered his face with the pillow again, and pulled the lid back sharply.

There was a sharp explosion; a flash; a billowing cloud of grey smoke.

Although he had half expected something of the kind, Rollison darted back, letting the lid bang down; it closed upon a tongue of flame. He banged against the wall, recovered, and saw the smoke curling out of the sides of the case, and dispersing in the room. He strode into the bathroom, dropped the pillow into the bath and turned both taps on, waited until the pillow was soaked, then hurried back to the bedroom.

Smoke and flame were forcing their way from the sides of the case, and the room seemed very hot. He stood back, putting his right foot up against one of the clasps and gradually opening the case; flame stabbed and roared. He got the lid into a position where he could toss it wide open, kicked, and dropped the soaking pillow on to the burning clothes. There was a hiss, and a spitting kind of roar, followed by a cloud of steam and smoke.

Three carafes of cold water later, the fire was out.

Rollison picked up the smaller, undamaged case, put all Lola's things he could find inside, locked it, then went out. He closed the door quickly, for the stench of burning might raise an alarm. The door was self-locking. He hurried to the lift and downstairs, then went to a call-box and dialled Whitehall 1212. When Scotland Yard answered he asked for Superintendent Grice, but Grice was not in.

"I think you ought to send to Room 517, at the Rol-chester Hotel," Rollison said to an Inspector. "Some kind of fire bomb was let off inside a suitcase."

"But who——?"

"Tell Mr Grice that Rollison called," Rollison said.

He rang off, and went out of the telephone box, carried the suitcase across to the porter and asked the man to get him a taxi. Five minutes later he was driving along Park Lane, with the stench of burning still in his nostrils, and something even more vivid in his mind.

What would Lola Davenport's face have looked like if she had opened that suitcase, and taken the full force of the explosion? She would have been disfigured for life, and probably blinded, too.

There could hardly be an uglier thought.

When Grice heard of it, he would take even more vigorous steps than usual: once he had been injured and nearly blinded by the same kind of beastly trick.

That had been in the heyday of Gus Blacker, who was dead enough to leave the Toff a country house and Lola Davenport a fortune.

7

SLEEPING BEAUTY

As Rollison turned into Gresham Terrace, he saw a sight familiar to him but remarkable to many: a T-Model Ford, painted sky-blue, every piece of metal shining as if it were the most modern of chromium, the windows gleaming, the whitewall tyres looking brand new. This vehicle was parked outside Number 22; a small group of teen-agers, to whom Model-T was as antediluvian as a gramophone with a horn, were pressing close to it. But they were not touching it, for sitting at the wheel was a small man with big ears and a bald head; a very ugly little man named Charlie Brane. As Rollison stepped out of his taxi, Charlie's face expanded with a broad and toothy smile, and the group round the car turned to see what had caused this.

Charlie thrust open the door and jumped down, proving to be so short that he barely reached Rollison's shoulder. But the clasp of his huge hand was like steel calipers, and he pumped Rollison's arm with the vigour of a dynamo.

"Glad to see you agen, Mr Ar! Gotta bitta funnangames f'rus?"

"Could be, Charlie," said Rollison. "How's Lady Maude?"

"Lady Maude, cor, that's a good one, that is. Cor strike me, wait till I tell her, she'll be in fits! Fancy you remembering that. Cor . . ." He was trying not to double up with laughter at Rollison, under the startled gaze of the spectators.

The front door was open. Rollison went in, and saw a taller, thinner man than Charlie, wearing blue denims and a choker, studying the array of electricity meters in a passage alongside the stairs. This was Mick Downall, bosom friend of Charlie Brane, and one of the most loyal supporters of Bill Ebbutt, who owned the Model-T. Ebbutt also owned a pub and a gymnasium in the East End, and was plagued by a Salvation Army wife and a conscience.

Rollison, his heart lighter now that he knew how quickly Jolly had set to work and how promptly Ebbutt had responded, hurried up the stairs. Although the front door of his flat was closed, he could hear Ebbutt's deep yet wheezy voice. This time Jolly was on the alert, and the door opened.

"That Mr Ar?" Ebbutt was eager, and he pushed forward as Jolly stood aside; a man six-feet tall and more, with a huge girth, although still as hard as nails, three chins, and a conical shaped head. He also crushed Rollison's hand. "Strike me, Mr Ar, it's good to be on duty again, it is, take it from me. How are yer? You'd never believe it, the boys had to draw lots. When they heard what was on, eleven of 'em wanted to come up West, so drawing lots was the only fair way to deal with the sitooation, weren't it?"

"Yes, Bill. How's Lil?"

"Lil's in the pink, as usual. Mr Ar, what's this about Gus Blacker? He's bin kicking up the daisies for a coupla days or more."

"Sure, Bill?"

"Mr Ar," wheezed Ebbutt, "you've 'ad some queer ideas in your time, and I ain't saying a lot of 'em 'aven't bin justified, but Gus Blacker's dead an gorn, you can take it from me. I was at the funeral. Don't get me wrong. I didn't go to pay any respects to the dead, I just went to say good riddance."

"Did you see him after he died, Bill?"

"Now, Mr Ar——"

"Did you?"

"Well, I never exactly *saw* the corpus, but you know old

Chalky White? He's gotta job with Mason's, the under-takers, and *he* saw Blacker. Said 'e looked as if he was just going to bust a bank, or else wondering what the dames were like where he was going to."

Rollison chuckled.

"It sounds all right, Bill."

"Mr Ar, Gus Blacker's dead, and don't let no one tell you nothing different."

"All right, Bill." They had been moving as they talked, and were now in the big room, where Ebbutt stood for a minute, looking at the Trophy Wall and probably reflect-ing on the fact that he had helped the Toff in at least half the cases which had left their mark there. "Did Jolly tell you anything else?"

"Not a blinking word."

"Would you like tea, sir?" inquired Jolly.

"Cuppa char'd go down a treat," accepted Ebbutt. "Now, what's on, Mr Ar? Blacker bin striking at you from the grave? Be just like him, that would."

"What do you know about his last few years on earth, Bill?"

"Made a fortune, that's the truth about Blacker," said Ebbutt, gloomily. "It's always the blooming same, there's no justice in this world. He musta retired with a hundred thousand nicker, and then he starts playing the Stock Exchange and the gee-gees, and gets everything bang on the nose. I heard he was worth half a million quid when he died."

"Who told you?"

"Ticky Mendelsohn, his accountant," said Ebbutt promptly. "At least, Ticky didn't tell me, close-mouthed Ticky is, but 'is daughter Ethel's young man is Ben's chief clerk, and he told a pal 'oo told Lil——"

"It was true," said Rollison.

Ebbutt said: "Arf a million *quid*?"

"More, Bill."

"The flicking end, that is," complained Ebbutt, bitterly.

"There's certainly no justice in this world, Mr Ar, no justice at all. Half a million—'ere, you're pulling my leg."

"I saw his will and the figures this morning."

Ebbutt moved, as if dazed, until within reach of the hempen rope, and began to play with it between his fingers, giving the impression that he could not have had worse news. When he spoke, it was with a wheezy kind of resignation.

"Beats the band that does, Mr Ar. Half a million nicker and no one to leave it to. What a blinking shame. When I come to think of all the people 'e swindled who could do with a few hundred—who *did* he leave it to, Mr Ar?"

"I'll show you," said Rollison. "Keep quiet, Bill. I want you to take a good look." He led the way out of the living-room and to the door of the guest room; picking a lock with a picklock was as easy to him as turning a key. He listened intently at the door, heard nothing, and opened it an inch or two.

Lola Davenport had kicked off her shoes, loosened her skirt, lain down, and gone to sleep. She lay a little to one side, knees slightly bent upwards, an eiderdown askew across her body. Her head and shoulders were in full view from the door, and Rollison felt again the strange, almost mesmeric effect of her beauty. It was as if she could disarm suspicion, and melt all resistance away. The woman of the world, the night-club queen, the woman hated by at least three wives, looked like a little child. Her repose was so complete that there was no doubt that she was fast asleep.

Ebbutt's breath was whistling through his nose. Rollison glanced at him, saw how wide open his eyes were, saw his parted lips. He judged the moment when Ebbutt had seen enough, then backed away and closed and locked the door.

"Well, wot do you know!" Ebbutt muttered. Dazedly,

he led the way back to the big room. "Well, how about—
say, Mr Ar."

"Yes, Bill?"

"Know what I think?"

"What do you think?" inquired Rollison, feeling the
sparking of hope that Ebbutt would be able to shed light
on the mystery of Lola.

"There's only one name for her," declared Ebbutt.
"Sleeping Beauty, that's what she is. The Sleeping Beauty
herself." He spoke as if he had just then invented the
name.

"Very apt," said Rollison, smoothly covering his disappointment. "Ever seen her before?"

"Nope."

"Seen anyone like her?"

"There can't be no one like her," declared Ebbutt
fervently.

"Think hard, Bill."

Ebbutt frowned so much that he brought his eyes
together in a squint, made a deep groove between them,
and corrugated his forehead. He was still concentrating
like this when Jolly brought in the tea, with wafer-thin
bread and butter and some cream cakes of the kind which
Ebbutt adored. Jolly poured out the first cups, and went
off. Ebbutt gulped down a cup of tea as Rollison sipped,
and then sat back and declared:

"It's a fact, Mr Ar. I've never seen no one like her."

"She could be Gus Blacker's daughter."

"Not by no woman I knew, I shouldn't think. She——"
Ebbutt was in the act of stretching out for a cake when he
stopped as if paralysed, and peered at Rollison with dis-
belief glinting in his eyes. "You trying to tell me Blacker
left her *all* that dough?"

"Most of it, Bill."

"Well I'll be——" began Ebbutt, gulped, picked up a
cake with a surprisingly dainty movement, and spoiled this
by popping it into his mouth whole. It was almost im-

possible to hear him saying: "*Mmmmmm.*" Then he shook his head and went on: "Who is she, apart from who she might be?"

"One of the most celebrated night-club performers in the United States."

"Can't say I'm surprised about that," declared Ebbutt. "She'll knock everyone cold. I know one thing, I got to change those men. Mick Downall's got to leave here quick, he wouldn't never keep 'is eyes off her. Yankee, is she? Well that don't surprise me neether. Blacker used to go to Noo York most years. Said he had business there. How about this, Mr Ar—could she ha' bin his floosie?"

"She says she wasn't."

"I never liked disbelieving a lady," Ebbutt reflected. "Well, strike me!" He took another cake, and masticated absentmindedly. Then some kind of problem occurred to him again, and he began to rub his chin. Rollison poured out more tea. "Listen, Mr Ar," said Ebbutt, "what's she doing at your place?"

"She says someone tried to kill her in New York and she felt she needed protection in London."

"Kill *that* bit of all right? They must be crazy!"

"She booked in at the Rolchester," Rollison went on, and explained exactly what had happened. The effect upon Ebbutt, as well as upon Jolly, who had come in to replenish the hot-water jug, was quite astonishing. Ebbutt's mouth began to drop open and his eyes to round; then slowly his mouth closed and his lips tightened, while Jolly stood with the hot-water jug in one hand, staring down at Rollison. When he had finished, Ebbutt said thinly:

"That's just what Gus Blacker useter do."

"The same thing precisely," said Jolly.

"*Blimey!*" exclaimed Ebbutt, getting his second wind.

"But Blacker's dead, remember," Rollison said.

"Wouldn't stop 'im from teaching someone 'is tricks, Mr Ar—before he died, I mean. Strewth!" Ebbutt turned towards the door and seemed to be attempting to look through walls and doors. "If Sleeping Beauty had opened the suitcase she would have got that lot in her face, then."

"That's what it seems like, Bill."

"It's a wicked shame!"

"Did you—did you inform Superintendent Grice?" inquired Jolly, in a low-pitched voice. "He was once nearly blinded by a similar booby-trap."

"The Yard should be at the Rolchester by now. I phoned them," reported Rollison. "See why we needed you and your chaps, Bill?"

"You betcher I can see. Well, this beats the lot. Don't spring no more surprises at me today, will you, Mr Ar? I couldn't take no more."

Rollison murmured: "Not even a little one, Bill?"

Ebbutt regarded him suspiciously. Jolly refilled the hot-water jug and went off, as if wanting to commune with himself. The quiet of the apartment seemed greater than it had that morning. Ebbutt was sitting there with his enormous paunch protruding, and several of his favourite cakes lying unheeded on the dish in front of him. Then he smoothed his hand over his head, and said:

"Let's have it straight."

"Gus remembered me in his will," announced Rollison, and paused long enough for Ebbutt to recover. This time the news was really too much for Ebbutt. After a minute, he pushed his chair back, stood up, dabbed his forehead with his handkerchief, and padded to the window. Rollison went on with the story in some detail, partly to make sure that Ebbutt knew everything, partly to get it all clear in his own mind. When he had finished, Ebbutt came back to the table, picked up a cake absent-mindedly, ate it, and said:

"So now you gotta n'ouse."

"A country house, Bill."

"Let me tell you something, Mr Ar—you keep away

from that place. Don't you go nowhere near it. If Gus Blacker left you anything in his will, he did it so as ter get his own back on you. It'll blow up under you, or catch fire, or else the walls are imprigenated with some disease—that's for sure. Take it from me, Mr Ar, you've got to turn that legacy in." Ebbutt looked up, and saw Jolly hovering. "You hear that, Jolly? Mr Ar's got to turn that 'ouse in. You've got to make sure 'e do. The three thousand a year's the sweetener. Blacker did that to make sure that you wouldn't turn it down flat, don't you agree, Jolly? The one sure thing is—keep away, Mr Ar. Put it on the market, blow it up or burn it down, but don't you go nowhere near it."

Ebbutt stopped in front of Rollison, and stood glaring down in an attitude almost of menace.

"I wish very much that you would take Mr Ebbutt's advice," said Jolly.

8

MORE ADVICE

EBBUTT stood on one side and Jolly on the other, staring down at Rollison as if commanding him to take their advice. After a few seconds, the telephone bell began to ring. Jolly glanced at it, but did not move immediately, and the ringing went on and on.

Rollison felt a flare of annoyance, but did not show it as he murmured: "She's really put you off your stroke, Jolly, hasn't she?"

"I beg your pardon, sir." Jolly turned immediately and hurried to the telephone; the ringing sound was cut off, and he announced: "This is the Hon. Richard Rolli-sidence." Ebbutt was looking at Rollison with that ....and. There was nothing remotely comic a....... he meant exactly what he said, so he was very w......

"One moment, please," said Jolly. "It is Mr Grice's office, sir."

"Ah," said Rollison, and stood up as Ebbutt muttered: "Gricey will teach you some sense." Rollison stifled a feeling of irritation with Ebbutt, and took the telephone.

A crisp-voiced man said: "Mr Rollison?"

"Yes."

"Mr Grice asked me to say that he is calling on you about five o'clock, and will be glad if you will stay in."

"Ah," said Rollison again. "I'd like to see him. Thanks. Where is he?"

"At the Rolchester Hotel."

"I'll wait for him," Rollison promised. He put down the receiver, and moved so that he could handle the plumber's hammer on the Trophy Wall. "Everything's bright with spit and polish," he remarked. "I'll go out another morning. I—Jolly."

"Sir?"

"We've forgotten Algoa Prendergast!"

"You asked me to make a note that we would discuss that matter tomorrow morning."

"I said later this morning," Rollison declared, irritably. "Send him his cabled thousand, and ask him to send us a monthly report on the claim." He took the rope and began to swirl it round and round, like a lasso, annoyed with himself for his difficult mood. He noticed Jolly go out, as if resentfully. "Brings back a lot of memories, doesn't it, Bill?" he made himself go on.

"That ought to have been pulled tight round Blacker's neck. He wouldn't have been able to play this kinda game if they'd 'ung 'im," Ebbutt declared. "What's this 'ouse like, Mr Ar?"

"Gammon and Hanbury said that they would send a photograph and some plans round," said Rollison. "They should be here by now. What have you arranged with your chaps, Bill? Two at the back, two at the front and two up here while Lola stays?"

"Lola?"

"The Sleeping Beauty."

"That's right," said Ebbutt, and added meaningly: "So long as you stay around Gresham Terrace, we can look after you. You'll be all right in the West End, too. But if you go anywhere outside the boundaries of the West End I can't guarantee nothing, Mr Ar."

"I'm not worried much about me," said Rollison, sharply. Didn't they think he could look after himself?

He moved to the desk, took up an AA book, flipped over the pages, and turned to Sandro: it was given as a village with a population of 908 souls. He traced it on the map as between Winchester and Basingstoke, on a side road, and as Ebbutt breathed on the pages, there was a ring at the front door bell. Rollison glanced up. A green light showed above the door, which meant that Jolly had already approved the caller. Rollison went to the room door and looked into the lounge hall. Jolly was opening the door; he must have been near when the caller had rung. Above the lintel of the door was a periscope mirror, and in this Rollison or Jolly could see whoever had called.

This was a young man carrying a large flat parcel; George Hanbury, in fact.

* * *

"I brought these myself, Mr Rollison, because I was so eager to know what more you could tell me about Miss Davenport," said Hanbury. "Are you sure that she has been seriously ill? She sounded perfectly all right on the telephone from New York, and nothing she said indicated that she wasn't well."

"She's much better than she was," Rollison assured him.

"Can you be sure?"

"Yes."

"It's a remarkable thing," said Hanbury, as if baffled. "I reserved a room for her at the Rolchester Hotel, and checked with the airport that her plane was in. Then I rang the Rolchester. She checked in, as the Americans say, and went out again immediately. I suspected that something a little peculiar had happened. There was a remarkable change in the tone of the operator's voice when I asked for Miss Davenport. She hasn't been taken ill again, has she?"

"No."

"Mr Rollison," said Hanbury, as if questioning a witness, "how can you be positive of that?"

"Because she's talked to me on the telephone," said Rollison. "And she will be in touch with you tomorrow. Now, can we have a look at this house?" He was brusque.

"Well . . ." began Hanbury. He kept talking about Lola Davenport as he untied the string from the parcel.

Ebbutt and Jolly stood close enough to see, and Ebbutt drew in a rattling breath when he saw the photograph of the Manor. Hanbury stood back from it, enthusing. Rollison picked it up and stood it on the back of a chair, against the wall. They crowded round in a half circle, admiringly. Then Hanbury handed out some smaller, glossy prints of the grounds. Ebbutt's eyes were popping before he had seen them all.

"And here are the actual plans of the house, from blue-prints which were drawn up, I understand, when central heating was put in at Mr Blacker's instructions, about five years ago. They show every detail, Mr Rollison. Here you see are the main rooms—magnificent rooms. Three of them are thirty feet by forty feet! Two, the dining-room and the drawing-room, have Adam fireplaces. There is a ball room . . ."

"More like a blinking pitcher palace," Ebbutt declared. "What's any man want with a place like that these days, Mr Ar?"

"More to the point, what did Blacker want when he bought it?" asked Rollison, and then looked round as there was another ring at the door. Jolly, still subdued, went across to check and then to open the door. A minute later Rollison heard Grice's voice.

Grice came in; a tall, sparely built man, with a sallow skin and a white mark at the bridge of the nose, where the skin was stretched so tightly. His eyes were brown, his hair was brown flecked with grey, and he was dressed in a perfectly-fitting brown suit. As he turned to look at Ebbutt, he revealed to Rollison that big burn scar at the side of his face—caused not by Blacker, but by someone who had worked with Blacker.

"Well, Rolly," he greeted, heavily.

"Hallo, Bill. You don't know Mr George Hanbury, do you?"

"I don't think we've met, but I've often seen your photograph," said Hanbury, and shook hands eagerly.

Then he looked from Rollison to Grice, as if he could not be sure what to say next. "Is—ah—could—ah—has this visit anything to do with Gus Blacker?" he demanded.

"Mr Hanbury is a partner in the firm of solicitors acting for Blacker's estate," explained Rollison.

"I see," said Grice. "I wish——"

"I was saying to Mr Rollison this morning that it has been most refreshing, most revealing, to realise that towards the end of his life Mr Blacker had such a change of heart," said Hanbury.

"Change of heart?" echoed Grice.

"He didn't 'ave no 'eart to change," asserted Ebbutt roundly.

"Now, really——" began Hanbury.

"Bill, I think we'd better tell Mr Hanbury what has happened," said Rollison, and he turned to the young solicitor. "Miss Davenport was twice attacked before she left New York, and once attacked since she arrived in London. A high explosive was hidden in one of her suitcases; if it had exploded in her face she might have been killed and would certainly have been disfigured and blinded. We don't yet know what it's all about, but we do know that Blacker used the same kind of methods when he was operating in London."

"Attacks on her *life*," breathed Hanbury.

"So it appears."

"Good gracious me!" gasped Hanbury. "I don't understand." He stared at Rollison. "But I do understand now why you told me that she had been ill. She—Mr Rollison! Is she safe? Is she *safe*? I must ask for protection—police protection. I must ask——" He began to splutter.

"She's getting good protection since the attack at the hotel," Grice assured him. "I don't think you need worry about her for today, Mr Hanbury. Now I wonder if you will mind if I ask Mr Rollison a few questions privately?"

"Oh. Oh, yes, of course, of course. I must be getting back to the office, in any case. There are a few letters to sign, and we are still so short staffed. Poor Mrs Regson will be distracted. But I was so anxious to be sure that —*is* Miss Davenport safe?"

"Yes. If you will just wait for a few minutes," said Grice, and moved towards the hall door. Rollison followed him. As they left the big room, Grice demanded:

"Is the woman all right?"

"Perfectly," Rollison assured him.

"Do you think this chap ought to be followed? I'll lay a man on, it won't take long."

"I'd wait a bit," advised Rollison, and appreciated Grice's reason for having this word in private. "I'd rather he didn't know that Lola's here, though."

Grice said: "All right."

When they went back into the big room, Hanbury was peering out of the window. He swung round, and burst out immediately:

"Where *is* Miss Davenport?"

"Just at the moment I don't want anyone to know," said Grice, firmly. "She has been attacked, as you've been told, and the fewer people who know where to find her, the better, for the time being. I'll inform you immediately it's considered safe, and in any case you will hear from us by the morning."

"Oh," said Hanbury blankly. "I see. Well, in that case——" He hesitated, then put his right hand to his pocket and took out a large envelope. He shook a photograph out of the envelope and held it towards Rollison. It was a picture of Lola, and a remarkable one, because— except for the wispiest of brassières, two tiny glittering stars, at each breast, and a sparkling loin cloth—she was wearing nothing at all. Her head was thrown back, her lips parted, and there was a look in her eyes so seductive, so sensuous, so overladen with sex, that it was hard to believe that the camera could catch such an expression.

"You mean that someone nearly disfigured *her*?" Hanbury gasped.

"Yes," said Grice, flatly.

"The creature must be mad—*must* be mad," declared Hanbury. "It's a great shock, very great indeed. You will put me in touch with her at the earliest possible moment, won't you?"

"I will," promised Grice.

Jolly showed Hanbury out, and closed the door firmly behind him. Grice moved his position so that he could see the picture of Sandro Manor more clearly. When he had spent some time studying it, he glanced at the photographs and the plans. Jolly did not come back into this room, but stayed in the domestic quarters.

"Mr Grice," said Ebbutt, "Jolly and me want to make sure that Mr Ar never sets foot in that place, but if I know the meaning of the look in his eyes, it's a waste of time. Can't you stop him?"

Grice said: "I don't know yet." He looked broodingly into Rollison's eyes, and he was not smiling. "I hope so. You know what would have happened to Miss Davenport, Rolly, don't you?"

"It did dawn on me."

Grice said: "I've had an expert examining the burned clothes and the case. He tells me that if that had exploded into the woman's face, she would have been rendered unconscious on the instant. If the fire had not been put out quickly, the room would have become a mass of flames, so the woman would have been burned to death, and there would have been a serious fire at the hotel. I take it you put the fire out?"

"Yes."

"And I take it you see what it means."

"What it could mean."

"It means that there is acute danger both for you and for Miss Davenport," declared Grice. "And it also means that Blacker laid extremely careful plans before he died. Remember that Blacker knew you as well as you knew him. He realised exactly how you would react to a challenge like this. He knew that your natural impulse would be to go and find out what he had done at the house, and would be quite sure that the knowledge of an attractive young woman in danger would distract you at the same time. I knew Blacker too, remember. I'm quite sure that he planned to kill you, through this legacy, and I'm equally sure that if you even visit this house, you will be inviting sudden death."

"Oh, come," protested Rollison.

"I mean it. If it were possible for me to give you orders I would order you not to accept this legacy."

Rollison felt a surge of annoyance; everyone seemed to want to order him about today, and for some reason it irritated him more than it should.

"I see what you mean," he said. "But I don't think I like the idea of refusing a challenge from Blacker, even from behind the veil."

"Now, Mr Ar——"

"You cannot possibly believe that Blacker would fail to make foolproof arrangements," Jolly pleaded from the door, and as Rollison looked up he came in further, saying: "I am sorry if this morning's events have unsettled me, sir, and very much regret if I am presuming too much, but—this situation frightens me. It really does."

"Puts the wind right up me," wheezed Ebbutt. "What I can't understand is why he leaves that strip-tease floosie half a million quid, and then tries to do her in before she's got her hands on the dough. It don't make no sense to me."

"Now isn't that a very remarkable thing," said Lola Davenport, from just behind Jolly; and she made all the men swing round and gape. "Because I can't understand why he should do such a thing for this floosie, either." She smiled sweetly at Ebbutt, who was so embarrassed that his cheeks turned pink. "In fact I don't believe that he would. I don't believe he would plan any injury to me. Nor do you, Richard, do you?" She moved past Jolly, smoothly, smiling at him as she passed. "You don't think you're fighting a man behind the veil, do you? You know that you're after someone who hates you as much as Gus obviously did."

She reached Rollison's side, and took his arm.

"If you don't think that, Richard, I'm going to be very disappointed in you."

9

JOKE OF A DEATHTIME

ROLLISON glanced swiftly away from Lola to Grice and
Ebbutt, who were side by side. Both showed an instan-
taneous reaction, Grice simply with a stiffening of his lips
and a clenching of his hands, Ebbutt much as he had when
he had seen the woman in the bedroom.

She had looked lovely then. Now she was so beautiful
that it hardly seemed possible anyone could look so flaw-
less. She had brushed her hair back carelessly from her
forehead, and made up a little—also carelessly, or else
casually. She was smiling. The huge collar of the coat of
her suit was raised so that it made a kind of frame for her
face.

Before anyone spoke, she turned towards Ebbutt, held
out her right hand, and said:

"So you're Superintendent Grice. I'm very happy to
meet such a famous individual, Superintendent."

Ebbutt's right hand went forward slowly, as if of its
own accord. He did not correct her. She took his fingers,
and he gave a convulsive kind of gulp, snatched his hand
away, and darted back—as if from something deadly.

"I'm—*I'm* not Grice," he choked.

He had given Grice the few moments' grace needed to
recover from the shock of seeing Lola; now Grice looked
her up and down as if dispassionately, as Rollison said:

"A very natural error, Lola—but this is Superintendent
Grice."

"Why, I'm so *sorry*," Lola breathed, and turned to
smile languorously at Grice, as if determined to destroy
his stern composure. "You're so well-dressed, Superintendent, it simply did not occur to me that you could be
the policeman."

71

This time, she did not offer to shake hands.

Rollison said: "Lola, I'd like you to meet Mr Ebbutt, a very old friend of mine and an old adversary of Gus Blacker. Mr Ebbutt's friends are here to act as your bodyguard."

"*And* Mr Ebbutt himself?"

"Er—sure, if I'm wanted," Ebbutt croaked.

"Why, that's wonderful, just wonderful!" declared Lola, and gave a smile which could not have been more lingering had she been trying to seduce a millionaire. "I do hope you will forgive me for eavesdropping, but I woke up and heard men's voices—I never could resist men's voices."

"Or even just men?" murmured Rollison.

"Now, Richard, that wasn't very gracious of you."

"Miss Davenport, did you hear what happened at the Rolchester Hotel?" Grice demanded.

"Why, yes, I did."

"I hope you realise that this indicates very great personal danger to you."

"I certainly do. That's why I asked Mr Rollison for help."

"Why didn't you come straight to Scotland Yard?"

Lola considered, and then gave a reasoned answer.

"I didn't think that Scotland Yard would be interested in what nearly happened to me in New York," she said, "and I had such great confidence in Mr Rollison. After all, I didn't know about the fire bomb in my suitcase until I heard you talk about it. Richard, I want to thank you for what you did—I know that I owe my life to you. I'll never forget that."

That sounded as sincere as the simple thanks of a child. The seductiveness faded from her expression; she looked at him as if she really intended to show gratitude for the rest of her life.

"Always glad to be of service," murmured Rollison.

"I hope it won't be necessary to perform that service for

me again," said Lola, and now she turned a speculative gaze upon Grice. "Superintendent, why are you so sure that it would be dangerous for Mr Rollison to go to this house which he has inherited?"

"Unless you know the history of the conflict between Mr Rollison and Blacker, I don't think you would be able to understand," Grice replied.

"I might possibly surprise you with my grasp of the situation," Lola retorted sweetly.

"We don't want none of this beating about the bush," Ebbutt interpolated; to Rollison's surprise he was scowling at Lola, as if at someone he disliked. Probably he had steeled himself to make sure that she did not make a fool of him. "Blacker's laid this game on, and the 'ouse is part of the trick. He always liked a practical joke, Blacker did—if you can call them jokes. He'd puncture a chap's tyre when he knew he was in a hurry. I've even known him fix a boat so that when his pals got into it, it sank under them. And this—you know what, Mr Rollison? This wouldn't be the joke of a lifetime, it would be the joke of a *death*time! There's a word for this kind of thing, mack something—you ought to know."

"Macabre," hazarded Rollison.

"That's it, mackarber. Right up Blacker's street, this would be, the joke of a deathtime." Ebbutt revelled in his phrase.

"Richard, the man who drove that Chev in New York was not a ghost," declared Lola firmly.

"The man who planted that booby trap in your suitcase wasn't, either," said Rollison dryly.

"Rolly, I know that I can't compel you to do anything, but I strongly advise you to refuse this legacy, and to have nothing to do with Blacker's estate," Grice said briskly. "Also, I strongly advise you not to help Miss Davenport. The police can and will give her full protection, and very soon we hope to find out who set that booby-trap. Miss Davenport, I will be glad if you will stay here until half-past six, by which time I shall have arranged for someone to follow you wherever you go. The officer will introduce himself to you, and you will be well advised to tell him where you're going, so that he can offer you the utmost protection. Ebbutt—" Grice swung round on the ex-prizefighter. "I can't give you orders, but you know that Blacker hated you almost as much as he hated Rollison. If you or any of your men get mixed up in this, you'll be asking for trouble."

"Don't I know it," Ebbutt muttered.

"Now I must get over to the Yard. There may be some news in about the man who planted that booby-trap," said Grice. "There were some prints on the side of the case which we don't think were Miss Davenport's or the porter's." He nodded to Lola, aloofly, and turned towards the door. Jolly appeared in time to open it for him, while Ebbutt stared gloomily at his back, and Rollison called:

"Keep in touch, Bill."

"Well, 'e's warned us, and that's flat," said Ebbutt.

"Do you always do what your policemen tell you?" inquired Lola, sweetly.

"I don't like fighting no ghosts," growled Ebbutt; then squared his shoulders and went on: "Oh, I won't let yer down, Mr Ar, but I've got to do one thing. I've got to tell the chaps who's behind this, and I can't be sure they'll all stay in."

"Perhaps I could persuade them," suggested Lola.

Ebbutt put his head on one side, stared at her, and gave Rollison the impression that he was determined at all costs to resist her influence. It was a curious fact that with both Ebbutt and Grice, Lola had created a kind of hostility after the first shock of seeing her. He had a curious feeling almost of depression, for this meant that the "mackarber" was making Ebbutt act out of character.

Then suddenly Ebbutt gave an expansive grin.

"You could make the boys stand on their 'eads, Miss, but once their wives got at yer, Gawd 'elp yer."

Lola looked startled; for a moment it seemed as if she was angry. Then, just as she had with Rollison earlier in the day, she began to laugh. The laughter seemed warm to Rollison and Ebbutt, and to be as genuine as it was deep. Ebbutt went on guffawing until he caught sight of the cream cakes. He picked one up, raised it to his mouth, then suddenly remembered his manners, put the cake into his saucer to free one hand, and picked up the dish.

"Try one of these," he said. "They're the tops."

"May I?" said Lola. She took one rather dubiously, nibbled at it as if making sure that the cream didn't smear her lipstick, and then took a big bite of the cake, and hesitated, her head raised. Then suddenly: "My, that's gorgeous!" she exclaimed. "I haven't tasted a French pastry as luscious as that since I was a child. Back home they all told me there was nothing so good as English cream, and I guess that's still absolutely true."

"Go on, take another," urged Ebbutt.

"I certainly will," said Lola, and as she picked up a cake, her eyes brimmed over with laughter. "If Jolly is going to feed me like this, Richard, I don't ever want to leave."

"Jolly's only been at half-steam so far," Rollison assured her.

"Richard," Lola said, after a long pause, "have you made up your mind what you're going to do?"

"No," replied Rollison. "I'm going to sleep on it; but I think I've an idea."

"I won't try to guess," decided Lola. "I like being kept in suspense."

"Tell you what," said Ebbutt gustily. "I'll go and 'ave a word with the boys, and find out 'oo wants to throw 'is 'and in, and 'oo's ready to 'ave a go. Shall I ring you later?"

"Ring me in the morning, Bill. We won't be going out tonight, and Grice's chaps can look after us for a bit."

"Suits me," said Ebbutt, and then turned and thrust

his right hand vigorously towards Lola. "I never meant no offence, Miss, and if you knew the way I 'ated Blacker's guts you'd understand 'ow I feel. But it ain't the men who worry me, it's their wives." He roared with laughter again. Lola managed to give the impression that the joke was still good with her.

"And we're going to have a cosy evening together, watching television, is that right?" she asked Rollison.

"Do you mind?"

"I'd just love it," Lola declared, as if there was nothing she wanted to do more.

*   *   *

A little after midnight, Rollison switched off the bed-side light, and turned over on his right side. It was co-incidence that this made him face the wall of the guest room, adjoining. Lola had started to yawn again soon after eleven o'clock, and she had been in bed for half an hour.

They had not talked about Blacker, or looked at the plans or photographs of Sandro Manor. Lola had re-laxed in an easy chair most of the evening, amused and entertained by the BBC programme, disappointed by the quality of the British commercials; she seemed to have put danger right out of her mind. No one telephoned. Out-side at the front was one of Grice's men. Another was stationed in the quadrangle at the back. Jolly had checked the locks and bolts at the doors, all of which had been specially designed to make the flat burglar-proof; it did not seriously occur to Rollison that anyone could break in.

It had been comparatively easy to push the main problem to the back of his mind, too, but he would soon have to decide what to do. He was almost sure that nothing would keep him away from Sandro Manor: he could never have resisted a challenge from Blacker in the old days, and there was a Machiavellian cunning about this which made it almost irresistible. He knew that the others were right to advise him as they had, but there was one factor which they probably did not understand; if he rejected this, he would find it hard to live with himself for a long, long time.

Of course, Blacker had realised that was how he would feel.

And, of course, Blacker had someone working for him.

Lola?

By stretching the imagination, it was possible to believe that, but Rollison doubted whether any of the others would think it likely.

Then it was someone unknown and so far unsuspected. The driver of a Chevrolet in New York City and at the airport; and a man who could get into her room at the Rolchester and who had access to that kind of cruel weapon.

This could be quite a battle.

He smiled vaguely to himself, yawned, and turned over. Gradually, Lola Davenport's face seemed to impinge itself on to his mind. He could picture her smiling; he could see her lying on the bed in the next room in an attitude of complete repose. She was very, very beautiful. She was so beautiful that she hardly seemed to be true. Could she be Blacker's daughter? Had she told the truth when she had denied being his mistress? It would be very difficult to be sure when she was telling the truth and when she was lying; Rollison had no doubt about Lola's cleverness.

He dozed.

Then, through the haze of sleep, he heard a sound.

He woke, as he had often woken in the past, with an awareness that something was wrong but without realising what it was. He listened. There was the sound again; a rustling. It seemed to come from the door. He was on his back, his head just high enough for him to look across the room, and had there been any light, he would have been able to see the door, but the night was pitch dark. He did not move.

The faint rustling came again. Now he was fully awake, and his heart was thumping, for he was aware of other dangers and of other fears. Could someone have broken in? If they had, was Lola safe? The temptation to fling himself from the bed towards the door was almost overwhelming, but if the intruder had a gun, he would have no chance at all. He had never known it so dark; never known so faint a sound and yet one so unmistakable.

Now the door was wide open, and he could discern the shape of the door frame, and a white form framed in it.

He knew, now, exactly what it was.

He kept very still, no longer with any sense of danger, because, if she meant him harm, Lola would do nothing in this flat. If he were to be killed or injured here she would be too obvious a suspect.

She was standing there, pushing the door. She closed it with a click which was very loud compared with the earlier sounds. Rollison thought that she was standing and staring at him; then there came another faint rustle of movement. She was coming towards the bed.

For the first time he moved, stealthily, so that his right hand touched the cord of the bedside lamp. He groped for the switch, and found it. It was a dim light, not powerful enough to read by, there simply against any emergency. Lola was much nearer him. He felt his heart thumping, he was almost choking—but there was not the slightest sense of fear. Lola knew just what she could do to a man, of course; she was like sex personified—and she was very, very close. He could smell a subtle perfume, which was almost like an incense, and which went to his head and seemed to overpower him.

He pressed the switch.

The dim light seemed very bright in this blackness. It startled Lola. She was just a few feet from the bed, wearing a short, diaphanous nightdress, little more than a pyjama jacket. Once she realized that he was awake she stretched out both hands, rather like a child, and after the momentary shock at being discovered, she began to smile.

10

QUICK TRIP

IF Jolly noticed anything even slightly amiss next morning, he showed no sign. If he noticed the slightest scent of perfume, he concealed it without effort. He moved the bedside light a few inches and put the tea-tray down, with the morning newspapers, then opened the curtains wider. Rollison, waking from a deep and heady sleep, was vaguely aware of what was happening, but took no notice. Finally, Jolly came to his side, and said:

"It's half past eight, sir."

Rollison grunted.

"I think you should wake up now," persisted Jolly.

"Am awake," grumbled Rollison. Already his mind was crowded with vivid memories of the night. "Anything happened?"

"Mr Ebbutt telephoned at eight ten, and promised to call again at nine o'clock."

"Hmph."

"The policeman in the street has been replaced by a man on day duty," Jolly went on. "That is a clear indication that Mr Grice thinks there is grave danger."

"Yes," agreed Rollison. "There's danger all right. Anything in the papers?" He struggled to a sitting position, then realised that his pyjama jacket was gaping. He ignored it.

"Each one carries the story of the fire at the Rolchester Hotel," said Jolly, "but the only thing they have in common is the fact that it happened in a Miss Lola Davenport's room, and that she has disappeared."

"Are we mentioned?"

"No, sir."

"Blacker?"

"There is some mention of the fact that Miss Davenport had recently inherited a large fortune, but no details are given."

"Hmm," grunted Rollison. "Better than it might be." He sat further up, and took the tea from Jolly's hand. With an unconcerned air, he inquired: "Miss Davenport up?"

"No, sir, and as it is not an American custom to have morning tea, I have not disturbed her. I thought that you might like a little time to think, before having to acquaint her with your decision."

"Yes," said Rollison. "Thanks. Have you reached any decision yet, Jolly?"

"Quite honestly, sir, I think that the decision has been made for us," said Jolly. He moved back a little. To Rollison he seemed rather older and more frail than he had the previous night, but his voice was steady. "Emotionally I am very anxious that you should refuse this legacy, but that course isn't practicable. I can see that. You are bound to be activated by a compulsion to go and see what Blacker has done there. Anything less would be——"

"Jolly," said Rollison, quietly, "you've done me a deal of good. Thanks."

"I cannot pretend to be happy about the prospect," said Jolly, "but then I have been unhappy at a lot of prospects in the past, and the reality has never proved as bad as I feared. This one is a little——"

"Macabre?"

Jolly smiled appreciatively, and went out.

Rollison stared at the closed door, and in spite of Jolly's understanding, unaccountably felt dissatisfied, almost irritable. He sipped tea, looked at the headlines of the newspapers, wondering how the news had leaked out. There were a dozen possible ways. He was surprised that even the *Globe* had missed the fact that Lola Davenport was such a nightlife celebrity in the United States. That puzzled but did not worry him. He poured out another cup of tea, put the cup down, and then noticed several long, dark curling hairs on the pillow. He raised one eyebrow, and stared at the door.

"Jolly," he said, "you get better all the time."

He finished the tea, got out of bed quickly, irritability forgotten, humming along to the bathroom for a quick tepid bath. He did not tap at Lola's door, but when he came from the bathroom she called out: "Rolly." He looked in. She was sitting up in bed with a fluffy bed-jacket round her shoulders and drawn up at the neck; the effect was quite indescribable. She looked—*innocent*. By her side was a tray with fruit juice in a small glass jug.

She waved.

"Good morning!"

"Good morning."

"Did you sleep well?"

"I had a perfect night."

"Why, isn't that just wonderful," said Lola. "Come and sit on the side of my bed and talk to me." She patted the bed.

"Sorry," said Rollison. "I've a lot of urgent decisions to make." He kissed his hand to her, and went on to his own room, blithely.

While dressing, he could just smell the odour of frying bacon; Jolly always began to cook breakfast when Rollison came out of the bathroom. He knew exactly what he was going to do, and the only question was whether to tell Grice. He had finished dressing and was by the dining alcove, when the telephone bell rang. He moved across to the desk and lifted the receiver.

"Rollison."

"'Morning, Mr Ar," said Ebbutt, bluffly.

"Hallo, Bill. How are tricks?"

"Not so bad, Mr Ar, not bad at all. Only two of the perishers have backed down. They don't want their 'appy 'omes broke up. And we've got a coupla new volunteers, coupla youngsters—Ted Clark and Phil Jacoby." Ebbutt paused, to give Rollison time to try to remember why the two names should be familiar; suddenly it came to him. Fifteen years ago, a man named Clark and another named Jacoby had been killed in an 'accident'—men who had worked with Gus Blacker, and who had quarrelled with him over the share-out of the spoils of three bank robberies. Their sons had been seven or eight at the time.

"They clicked?" demanded Ebbutt.

"Yes, I remember them," Rollison said heavily. "Are you sure they know the risks?"

"They know them all right—they always wanted to have a go at Blacker, but I kept 'em on the straight and narrer," declared Ebbutt. "Coupla promising boys in the ring, too. Then we're back at full strength, as the saying goes."

"Are they free to take a little holiday in the country?" inquired Rollison.

"I noo it, I noo it," said Ebbutt, with a chokey kind of laugh in his voice. "I told Gricey on the phone larst night, it would take more'n him and me and Jolly to keep you away from that manor. Now how about letting me and arf a dozen of the others go on ahead, Mr Ar? We could clear the place of booby-traps, p'raps, and——"

"Bill."

"All right, all right, it's a waste of time talking to you," said Ebbutt. Rollison felt a flash of annoyance, but Ebbutt seldom affected him that way; it must be his own mood.

"I'll tell you what I am doing, Mr Ar," Ebbutt went on. "I'm starting an inquiry into Blacker's past, finding out if he did have a kid who might 'ave gone to the States. If you ask me, London's littered with Blacker baskets, but——"

"It's a good idea, Bill."

"So long as you think so. I've told old Gricey 'e ought to 'ave a cut at the same thing, and if I was you, I would get me own lawyers cracking on it to find out more about Blacker. Because it's as near certain as can be that he had a crop of these little baskets, and he might have known one of them more than we realise. What I'm trying to say is this, Blacker may have an orfspring who inherited his worst side, and who might be as anxious to fix you as he was."

"I'll find out," promised Rollison, and quickly said good-bye. He was still a little out of temper with Ebbutt and with himself, but he forgot his mood when there was a movement at the door.

Lola appeared.

She wore the same skirt as yesterday, but a different blouse—of a jade green colour, cut so cunningly that it was impossible not to stare. She looked demure and rested as she floated towards the desk, both hands outstretched.

"Richard, I'm really hungry."

"We can soon fix that," said Rollison, "and we need a hearty breakfast before a trip into the country."

Quite suddenly, quite unexpectedly, Lola slid her arms round him, much as he had round her the day before, and kissed him with a fervour which was very close to passion. She held the kiss for a long time, and when she released him, took his right hand and led him towards the dining alcove and the breakfast table; it was as if she were already the woman of the house.

Jolly appeared a minute or two later, carrying a silver dish on which were eggs, bacon, sausages and kidneys. Lola's eyes glistened as they had at the sight of the cream cakes.

"Aren't I the luckiest person?" she declared. "I just don't have to worry about the calories. It doesn't matter how much I eat, I always stay around a hundred and forty pounds."

"And who can complain about that?" demanded Rollison.

*   *   *

"I was pretty sure that you'd go down there," said Grice. "But do it my way, will you?"

"How, Bill?"

"Go by a route which no one will suspect, and don't tell Ebbutt or even Lola Davenport just when you're going. At least have the sense to do that."

"Yes, Bill," said Rollison humbly. "Thanks. Now I've an idea too, if you and the Winchester chaps will play . . ."

When he had finished, he took a small box—matchbox size—out of a drawer, and looked inside. There were several little glass containers there, looking like phials of drug, actually of tear-gas. These made a very useful and effective weapon. He might need them before long.

As he put these carefully into his pocket, the front door bell rang, and in a moment, he heard Jolly's voice, followed by young Hanbury's. He did not want to spend time with the solicitor, and was frowning when Jolly came in.

"What's he after, Jolly?"

"He has brought a certificate which he wishes you to sign, claiming to be the Mr Rollison named in the will." said Jolly. "He appears to think that it will save some delay. I told him that you are about to visit the—ah—property, sir. He assures you that it won't take a minute and is a pure formality."

"Leave him in here while I go and get some cigarettes," Rollison said. "Tell him I won't keep him long." He passed the spare room, but did not speak to Lola, who was humming to herself, filled his cigarette case and primed his lighter, then went back to the big room. Hanbury, looking eager and faintly apprehensive, had the certificate ready to sign.

"And I hope you find the property very much to your liking," he said. "I feel sure you will."

*　　*　　*

Sitting at the wheel of his silver grey Bentley Continental, a recent acquisition, Rollison was acutely aware of the gracefulness of the car and the beauty of the woman next to him. Lola seemed as right in the passenger seat of the car as she did at Gresham Terrace. People turned to stare—not only men but women, not only men and women but youngsters, too. She had such a regal air.

Rollison knew that the Bentley could easily be traced but also that it had a speed no car on the road could match, unless it were one of the smaller sports cars, which he could pick out in a minute. He drove first through North London, and out to Hampstead, then cut across to the North Circular Road. Once the road was clear, he started to put on speed. Soon he swung under the overpass on to the Great West Road, and once he was out of the restricted area, put his foot down so hard that the car seemed to fly; and all the time, Lola seemed to purr.

Rollison surged past the airport as if challenging the turboprop aircraft warming up there, weaved his way towards and through Staines, then headed for Basingstoke and Winchester at a speed which seemed to leave all other traffic standing. Excitement shone in Lola's eyes.

Now and again Rollison looked into the mirror. When he reached the turn-off to Sandro, he said:

"No one's been on our tail, but they might have a reception party at the Manor."

"We'll soon find out, darling," said Lola.

"Lola," said Rollison, apologetically, "you aren't going to find out anything for a little while." He gave that statement time to sink in before continuing: "You're going into Winchester, where you're going to be the guest of the Hampshire police until I call through to say that it's all safe."

"Richard, you can't mean that." Lola sounded shocked.

"You're much too beautiful to take chances with," declared Rollison. "I don't have any choice."

She said angrily: "But you promised me——"

"Let me tell you a little secret," said Rollison. "We stop near the next village, which is on the way to Stockbridge, and you take on a police driver who will drive you into Winchester. I'll take his car, and borrow his uniform. Do you think that the hand from behind the veil will strike at a country copper having a look round?"

Lola was turning in her seat and looking at him; he was glad that he need not stay with her in this mood. He swung off the main road into a lane which widened out at the outskirts of a village. A black car with two men standing by it stood off the road. Rollison pulled behind them, and slid out of his seat.

"I'll send word as soon as I'm through," he promised.

"I hope you will," Lola said, and watched him as he walked away and one of the men, middle-aged and chunky, got in beside her. Rollison took a tunic from the man still by the black car, and then heard Lola call: "Richard, can you spare a moment?"

He went to her side of the car, pleasantly surprised that she had taken this so well. Her smile had a radiance which seemed to glow especially for him—until he was within arm's reach of her. She swung her arm and slapped his face hard enough to make him lose his balance; before he had recovered, she slapped him on the other side.

As he backed out of reach, he put his head on one side and said: "Now I'm not so sorry it was necessary. Driver, be careful, you're going to drive a dangerous explosive."

"I can tell," the driver said, and winked at Rollison as he drove off. Lola was still glaring.

*   *   *

Was she furious because of pique?

Or was it because this move did not fit into her own plans?

11

SANDRO MANOR

ROLLISON slid the police car to a standstill outside the
iron gates of Sandro Manor. He could not see the house
from here, but the grounds were in fairly good order, and
there were some magnificent trees. At one side, just inside
the gates, was a small old and weathered brick cottage
with a thatched roof which needed repairing or replacing;
at the windows were some clean curtains, but there was no
sign of movement. He got out of the car and approached
the gates, watching the cottage as well as the shrubs and
bushes; anywhere a man could hide.

The sun was hot and getting hotter. The grass and the
leaves were bright green from recent rains, and the birds
seemed determined to make the most of the sunshine
while it lasted. A blue dragonfly hovered near the
wrought-iron handle of the gates.

The uniform was of heavy blue serge, a little too large
for Rollison, but not uncomfortable. He wore his own
shoes. A pair of cheek pads inside the mouth made his
cheeks look plumper, and tiny rolls of cotton-wool in each
nostril made them look broader. Wearing the peaked cap
and the uniform, there was little risk that he would be
recognised.

He turned the handle, and the gates opened. They
squeaked as he pushed them back. He studied the cottage,
and as there was still no movement at the windows, went
back for the car and drove in. No one called out. The
drive curved round out of sight and he drove cautiously.
A cock pheasant appeared at one side, head up, colours
caught in glorious brightness by the sun; the hen was a
few yards away, half-hidden by the foliage of a spreading
cedar.

Rollison turned a corner and caught the first glimpse of
the house. It was built on a rise in the land, and sur-
rounded by lawns. Colourful creepers grew close to the
windows, robbing the brick walls of bareness. The empty
windows had a drab and dirty look, and as Rollison drew
nearer he saw that the white paint was dirty and flaking.
The first glimpse had shown the house as it could be; the
close-up showed it for what it was.

He pulled up on the square drive, close to a stone figure
of Cupid and what had once been a fountain; the basin
beneath it was littered with dead leaves. Some geraniums,
straggly and small, gave a speckled rash of colour in
flower beds which had been raked over fairly recently.

Except for the singing of the birds, there was no sound.

Rollison went to the front door. There was an old-
fashioned pull type bell, and he tugged it, but heard no
sound. He ought not to be surprised; Moody and his wife
were almost certainly at the back of the house, and so was
the bell: but the absence of any sign of the caretaker had a
curiously agitating effect.

Normally he would just take the situation as it came,
but now he felt a surge of irritation, rather as he had with
Ebbutt. What was the reason? Was Lola having this
effect on him? Was he worried deep down because of
danger to her—or because she might be involved?

Rollison walked back to the car and pressed the horn.
A dozen pigeons flew off two beech trees with a great
flapping of wings, and a covey of partridges rose out of the
uncut grass near the fountain, and went rustling away.

Rollison stepped back, to look at the top of the house,
but no one was at the windows of the first floor. He went
to the ground floor windows, and examined them; they
were fairly secure, but it would not be difficult for him to
open one.

He had taken it for granted that the caretaker would be
here, to admit the 'police'; now he had to decide what
Moody or anyone watching would think if a policeman

broke into the house itself. A genuine policeman was much more likely to walk round to the back.

Rollison went first to the south side, found closed french windows with the shutters drawn, and round the next corner, a garden door. Just beyond, a walled garden with an overgrown herbaceous border seemed a long way off. There were a lot of red brick out-buildings, and some old stables. He peered in at all the windows, experiencing a curiously flat feeling of anti-climax. The rooms were empty, and obviously in need of redecorating—it was exactly like any old empty house.

A gateway led to the domestic quarters, several rambling sheds and some single-storey buildings with tiled roofs. There was no sound or sign of movement until he turned a corner, when a big black cat stalked towards him. Rollison stopped abruptly.

The cat was plump and sleek; and after staring at him it turned away and went towards the walled garden.

"Looks well-fed," Rollison remarked to himself.

There was a short flight of steps leading to what looked like the back door; at the top was a bottle of milk. It was nearly one o'clock so why hadn't the milk been collected? Had the Moodys taken a day off? Rollison went up to the door, reminding himself that no one could possibly realise that he was Rollison: only Lola and a few policemen knew about this disguise. Yet he had the feeling which had been with him since the start of the affair: that he was being watched.

The door was locked.

This time, he took out his knife, opened a picklock blade, and worked very quickly. The lock was old fashioned and he turned it in less than a minute. He heard a padding sound behind him, loud out of the quiet, and spun round. It was the cat, which had jumped from a window sill. It seemed to glare at him. He pushed the door open wider, and the cat stalked past slowly, voluptuously, and disappeared.

The room beyond was an old wash-room, with two huge sinks, some brass taps, some buckets and brushes. Rollison kept reminding himself that the back door had been locked, and the milk hadn't been collected. Even if the caretaker and his wife had gone out for the day, they would have taken in the milk, surely.

He went into another room. This was an old-fashioned kitchen, in reasonably good repair. The huge cream-coloured Aga cooker was washed and clean. There was a smell of oil; a little oil cooking stove was under a window. In a corner was a larder, the door of which was ajar. Just under a table were two saucers, one with a little milk in it, one with the remains of some stewed meat. He touched the milk saucer with his toe; the milk was solid. So it had been there for some time. The cat rubbed against his legs. He opened the larder door, found a half empty tin of cat's food, rummaged round a drawer, forked some of the meat into the saucer, and saw the cat dart towards it as if it hadn't eaten for a long time.

"I'm glad I didn't bring Lola," he said aloud.

Every step he took seemed to be towards danger, although there was no real reason for thinking so. The silence was unnerving. He stepped into a passage where there was no sunlight; it struck quite chill. His footsteps echoed on bare boards. There was a sound as the cat banged the saucer against the wall. A door stood on the right of the passage, and daylight but no sunlight showed through. He reached this door and opened it wide.

The shock seemed to go through him.

A man and a woman sat in a big bed-sitting room, near the open window. Someone had used a hammer on their heads.

* * *

That was all Rollison found.

The blood spattered cushions and walls. The bodies were sitting as if they had been struck down while chatting to someone. Raincoats were draped over chair backs. A book lay on its face on the arm of the man's chair.

As Rollison stood there, he felt something rub against his legs, started, and looked down at the sleek cat weaving its way between his legs.

*   *   *

Rollison left without touching anything, but he carried with him a vivid picture of the battered couple, and of the hammer which lay on the floor by the side of the bed. It was exactly like the trophy on his wall.

He stepped out of the passage, into another, wider one which led to three small rooms, and a hall; the hall stretched from the front of the house to the garden entrance. His footsteps echoed, strange and eerie. He saw no other footprints. Nothing seemed to have disturbed the dust of the large rooms at the front.

He looked everywhere for a telephone, but found none.

He went slowly up the wide staircase, and around the gallery at the top. There were half a dozen main bedrooms, two with their own bathrooms; a third bathroom overlooked the walled garden. Next he went down a short flight of wooden steps to the servants' bedrooms. There was no odour except the slight fustiness one would expect of an empty house. He studied every door and every floor, and found most in perfect condition. One or two loose boards covered electric cables, that was all.

The wainscoting everywhere seemed sound; so did the picture rails in two of the main rooms.

When he had finished, he had been everywhere except up in the loft. He found the entrance to that above the stairs leading down to the servants' quarters, hauled himself up, and was greeted by a furious buzzing of flies, but five minutes satisfied him that nothing obvious was hidden up here; that there was nothing to fear.

He went to the edge of the hatch, to climb backwards down the ladder—and the ladder wasn't there.

Rollison had to remind himself that only a few minutes before he himself had climbed up it. He had not heard a sound. The flesh began to creep at the back of his neck as he strained his ears, but heard nothing. He could lower himself over the edge of the hatch, and drop down—but now he began to think of the rooms within sight—rooms and corners near which a man could hide.

He turned back into the loft, with the flies buzzing furiously at the leaded lights and around the electric lamp bulbs. He twisted two bulbs out of their sockets and returned to the hatch, then tossed a bulb in each direction, and before it exploded, swung himself down through the hatch, clung to the edge for a split second, and dropped. The bulbs exploded shatteringly as he was half-way down, and while he swayed to keep his balance he heard the tinkling of glass.

That was the only sound, once he had stopped moving; there was no sign of the ladder—which must have been moved to delay him if he needed to move quickly.

Very slowly and cautiously he went towards the main staircase, and looked at the front door. It was not bolted, simply latched. He pulled the knob of the latch back, and the door opened. At last he heard a sound—the sudden pop-pop-pop of a motor-scooter which must have been hidden in the bushes. A man's head and shoulders were disappearing down the drive, round the curve.

Rollison did not catch even a glimpse of the face, only of the black and white check cap. The engine sound was getting much softer; he stood there until he could hear nothing at all. He closed the front door, went to his car, and threw the bonnet up, checked that nothing had been tampered with, and got into the driving seat. The engine started perfectly. All the time he thought of Blacker, his love of practical jokes, his use of a plumber's hammer. He reached the curve in the drive, travelling slowly, and then felt the steering wheel wobble. He kept going for a few seconds, long enough to convince him that he had a flat tyre.

As he pulled up, it was almost possible to believe that he could hear Blacker laughing, fine head thrown back, mouth wide open, white teeth glistening.

That was simply imagination.

There was nothing fanciful about the dead caretaker and his wife.

*   *   *

There was an AA telephone box a quarter of a mile from the iron gates. Twenty minutes after Rollison left it, two police cars turned in at the drive. Sitting in the back of one of the cars was Lola.

*   *   *

"It's a hideous thing to happen," Lola said. "I'm really grateful to you for refusing to bring me here, Richard. I know that may sound insincere, but I promise you that I mean it. I would simply hate to see a dead person, and——"

She shivered; she looked very pale.

"Who do you think did it?" she asked, huskily.

"Not much point in guessing at that," Rollison said. He was back in his own clothes, and the Bentley stood outside the house. Two police cars were near it and another was at the back. The police had nearly finished their first investigation, and the two bodies had been taken off in an ambulance. The ladder found among the trees had proved clean of fingerprints. It was nearly half past five, and the late afternoon was very hot.

"The first question is—why should anyone do it?" Rollison went on moodily.

Lola looked as cool as if she were in an air-conditioned room.

"Would it help to know why?"

"It would help a lot," declared Rollison. "The peculiar

thing is that a double murder like this is likely to keep me away, not bring me here."

"Maybe they wouldn't think that would put you off."

Rollison said: "It makes absolutely certain that the police will be in possession for several days, and perhaps for several weeks. It means that the police are bound to search the house from top to bottom, have the floor boards up, go through every room with a comb, search everywhere they possibly can in the hope of finding a clue. So——"

He broke off.

"Richard! What have you thought of? Tell me what crossed your mind just then. I can see something did." Lola's cool fingers touched the back of his hand, the fingers which had stung his cheek so much a few hours ago. "Richard!"

"Something crossed my mind all right," said Rollison. "Blacker would have known that Grice and Jolly wouldn't be scared of what there might be at the house, and would search it. If he were alive Blacker would get the biggest laugh imaginable by making sure that the police had a kind of wild goose search. He would take it for granted that I would move in, even if I wasn't sure the place was safe from him."

Lola said: "You keep talking of Gus as if he was still alive."

12

HAMMER

"YES, I know," Rollison agreed soberly. "It's ludicrous." He slid his arm through hers. "Now that we're friends again, would you like to look round the house?"

She hesitated. "Do you want me to?"

"I don't think it will help and I'm sure the police would rather take the place to pieces without me being here. Let's go and have a drink and an early dinner, and come back afterwards. Grice will probably be around by then."

"Now that's a very good idea," agreed Lola with relief. "I could hardly eat a thing at lunch time, I was so mad at you and the policemen. Now I'm ravenous."

Rollison laughed. "We'll soon put that right."

He took her to the front of the house, where his Bentley now stood, watched by a young policeman whose gaze appeared to be one of yearning. The Superintendent from Winchester was obviously glad to see them go. Two more police cars had arrived, and the grounds were swarming with uniformed policemen, all searching for footprints. Four men were studying the tyre tracks, and some plaster casts were already being made.

Rollison drove to an inn deep in the New Forest, not far away, and Lola went into ecstasies over the thatched roofs, the timbered houses, and the ponies which ambled heedlessly across main roads as if motor cars were no longer lethal.

There was a fried Dover sole which melted in the mouth, Aylesbury duck and apple sauce with green peas and new potatoes, and strawberries and thick cream. Rollison saw Lola eyeing the big bowl of strawberries on the serving trolley almost longingly, and signed to the waiter to bring her more.

"Cream, madame?" asked the waiter.

"Surely, a whole pitcher of cream." She watched it being ladled on, and ate as if she hadn't had a meal all day. When she had finished, she covered Rollison's hand with hers and pressed gently. "You're forgiven completely," she declared.

"I'll tell you how I feel about you in the morning."

She laughed. "All right, Rolly! Do you know, back home my friends always said that England was a wonderful place but the food was terrible. Do you think they came to the same country?"

Rollison said: "Ask any Englishman, and he'll tell you that you can't get eatable food in the States, but I could take you to a gourmet's delight in a dozen cities."

"I bet you could," said Lola. "That was certainly wonderful. How long do you think we shall be at Sandro Manor?"

"Does it matter?"

"I was thinking, it would be very interesting to stop over for the night in this place."

"Then why not?" said Rollison. "They'll be able to rustle up a toothbrush." He went along to the desk and booked two rooms, then took Lola out to the Bentley where an earnest young man was telling an unbelieving young woman in a crash helmet that 'that car cost eight thousand pounds'. Lola looked thoughtfully at Rollison, and as he stretched out a hand with a key, she asked:

"Is that true?"

"Is what true?"

"Did this car cost nearly twenty-four thousand dollars?"

"There was a lot of tax," explained Rollison. Then he touched the keyhole with the key, looking down at her all the time; and he hesitated. With her quick sense of perception, Lola asked:

"What's the matter?"

"Go back to the porch," ordered Rollison quietly, and she obeyed without question.

No one else was nearby. The young couple were strolling like Martians towards their motor-scooter. Rollison saw the banners stuck to the big windshield, and recognised the American Automobile Association badge—AAA, without taking any notice of it. Very cautiously, he turned the key in the lock. Nothing happened. Lola didn't speak but he could sense the intensity of her gaze. He pushed the handle down very slowly. Still nothing happened. He stood nearer the bonnet of the car, away from the opening, and opened the door a little more quickly but still with great care. It was half open when Lola called:

"Is there anything to worry about?"

"We'll find out in a moment," Rollison said, and then a sports car roared past, and the motor-scooter started off, momentarily distracting his attention. He pulled a little more sharply. There was the crack of an explosion, a roar, a sheet of flame.

"*Richard!*" cried Lola.

He opened the door wider, then strode round to the boot, pulled it up carefully, snatched the fire extinguisher from its fitting, and raced back. Flames were already leaping high, and the upholstery was burning. He squirted evil-smelling foam over the door, the hinges, the floor and the seats, until the last traces of fire had gone. By the time he had finished, a crowd of a dozen or more people had gathered. Lola stood at the back, pale and silent.

Rollison satisfied himself that there was no further danger of fire, and refastened the extinguisher. When he came away from the boot, followed by questions such as: "How did that happen?" "What caused it?" he found Lola by his side. He picked up a roll of cheese cloth, and tore off a large piece. Lola took this from him without a word, went to the car and began to clean it. Rollison answered the various questions with the same stock answer: "I wish I knew."

Fifteen minutes later it was possible to sit in the car

without getting wet or dirty. Rollison spread a leather
travel rug over the seat, and slid in front of the wheel.
Lola came out from the hotel, after washing the dirt off
her hands.

"I've cancelled the rooms," Rollison said regretfully.
"We'll be safer in London."

"Richard."

"Yes?"

"Did Gus always use that kind of booby-trap?"

"Often. He used to think it funny."

"Did you see anyone at the car?"

"No. I saw some scratches and knew that the lock had
been forced."

"If you hadn't, what would have happened?"

"When you open the door of that car you face the
inside, and you're usually looking towards the hinge—it's
a natural attitude. I'd have got a lot of the blast in my face
and on my hands."

"Richard, who do you think——?"

"I don't know who, I've told you that," said Rollison,
and added savagely: "But before long I'm going to find
out."

*   *   *

He turned into the gates of Sandro Manor, waved in by
two policemen on duty. A crowd of thirty or forty people
had gathered about the gates with the aimlessness of
crowds at a place which has suddenly come into the news.
There was a familiarity about the grounds now, and
Rollison took the long curve faster than before. A red
shape appeared in front of him. He jammed on his
brakes as a little scarlet sports car came hurtling down the
drive towards him, its engine muffled by the trees. Sports
car tyres grated on the gravel and went up on the grass;
the Bentley stopped on the opposite side. There were two
or three feet between the cars.

Sitting at the wheel of the sports car was George
Hanbury.

It was hard for Rollison to know why he was so surprised to see the youth in the scarlet speedster. Partly, perhaps, because he hadn't associated the brisk but earnest and righteous young man with a love of speed; partly because Hanbury was dressed in the Continental black coat and the stiff collar and grey tie of the office, which was incongruous; and partly because the youth was here at all.

For a moment, Hanbury looked horrified. Then he shifted his gaze from Rollison towards Lola, and a greater transformation could not be imagined. Everyone was startled at seeing her; Hanbury looked astounded. Had he gazed upon an angel with wings coming down from the azure sky, he could not have been more impressed. His mouth not only dropped open, it looked as if it would stay that way.

Lola murmured: "Who is this gawk, Richard?"

"You be civil to him," said Rollison. "He's the solicitor handling Blacker's will, and Blacker's executor, and he can make a lot of difficulties for you."

"But he's still wearing his diapers!"

Rollison smothered a grin as he put his head out of the window, and called: "Think you could back thirty yards to the carriage way?"

Hanbury simply gaped at Lola.

"Mr Hanbury! Can you back a few yards?"

Hanbury gulped, glanced at Rollison, looked again at the woman, and then, as if to show that he was not quite so dumbstruck as he looked, he started the engine and put the car into reverse. It began to crawl back. Rollison noticed another thing; Hanbury reversed with the skill of the natural driver, in spite of his reaction to Lola. He drove the car into the wide neck of the drive near the house. Two plainclothes men came briskly towards him. Rollison drove past, and Hanbury's head turned round like a ventriloquist's doll being moved very slowly. Then he opened the door and got out, approaching Rollison, who also got out.

"Hallo," said Rollison. "What brought you?"

"I wished to inform the caretaker that you might want to inspect the property, and my senior partner authorised me to come down and make sure everything was in order," said Hanbury, in a stilted voice. He did not look away from Lola. "That—that is Miss Davenport?"

"Yes. Of course, you haven't met."

"Er—no," said Hanbury, hastily. "No, we haven't. Er—be good enough to introduce me, Mr Rollison, will you?"

"Mr Rollison," called one of the plainclothes men, "Mr Grice is in the house and would like to see you."

"Be there in half a minute," Rollison promised, and opened Lola's door. As she got out, he introduced the two much as if he was presenting a subject to a queen. Hanbury put out his hand, and Lola took it, held it lightly, and switched on the smile which she must know could turn blood to water.

"I'm very, very glad to know you, Mr Hanbury," she said. "I'm going to need your help very much."

Hanbury moistened his lips. "Anything—anything I can do. Pleasure."

"I'll be back in ten minutes or so," Rollison promised. Hanbury looked at him with such gratitude that it was almost pathetic. The two plainclothes men turned their backs on him, and grinned. Lola was still holding Hanbury's hand. Rollison and the others, one Yard man and one man from Winchester, walked towards the house. The Yard man, Detective Inspector Winter, chuckled on a rather high-pitched note.

"I wouldn't like my eighteen-year-old son to get within a mile of her," he remarked.

"I know what you mean," said the other man.

"You didn't lose much time sending for Grice," said Rollison.

"Obviously a Yard job, and his cup of tea," replied the Winchester man.

They went past a constable on duty at the porch and past three plainclothes men searching the hall. Some floor boards were up in one corner. Footsteps sounded overhead, and Rollison had the impression that a small army had taken over the Manor. They led him along the back passages towards the room where he had found the Moodys. Grice, a Winchester Superintendent, and two detective sergeants were there.

Grice was examining the hammer in the daylight near the window. A label had been tied to it, and obviously it had been tested for prints. He looked at Rollison, and gave a tight-lipped smile. It was obvious that he was badly shaken by what had happened here.

"At least you had the sense to send for us. I've known the time when you would have buried the bodies and pretended nothing had happened," he declared.

"A long, long time ago," defended Rollison, "and then only for a very good reason. Was the hammer the cause of death?"

"What makes you ask?" demanded Grice.

"No struggle, no sign that either of them moved, and unless there were two men, each with a hammer, one of the victims had to die first," said Rollison. "I guess that they were either drugged or in a drunken stupor when they were attacked."

Grice said: "We had a preliminary report in from the pathologist half an hour ago. They had taken sonoril, enough to put them into a dead sleep for eight or nine hours."

"Both killed with the same hammer?"

Grice said: "Yes. Yes, they were." He spoke in such a way that Rollison frowned across at him, and then looked hard at the hammer. The blood on the steel head had coagulated and was now a dull brown, instead of bright crimson as it had been when he had first seen it. "Time of death, about one thirty," said Grice. "Today."

"When I reached here?"

"Yes."

"There was a motor-scooterist," Rollison pointed out.

"Oh, yes," said Grice. "But we can't be sure what time he was here. There was a ladder, too, but we don't know when it was dropped over there among the trees. All we know for certain is that the Moodys were in a drugged sleep, and that they were then battered to death with——"

He broke off.

"That hammer," said Rollison.

"Your hammer," said Grice, very clearly.

"Don't be a fool," retorted Rollison. "It can't be mine."

"But it is," insisted Grice. "It is identical with Gus Blacker's hammer, used as an exhibit at his trial, and later released to you on permanent loan. When the hammer was described over the telephone, I suspected that it was your souvenir, and I went round to Gresham Terrace to check. It may seem remarkable, but Jolly hadn't noticed that the hammer from the Trophy Wall was missing until I pointed it out."

13

CLEAN BILL

Rollison moved across the untidy bedroom, and picked up the hammer. He had remarked on its similarity to the one which Blacker had used, but it had not occurred to him for a moment that it was the one from the Trophy Wall. On its shaft, however, there was a smooth patch and on this patch a number was engraved; that was the index number which Jolly had put on when he had put the hammer in place. Every trophy had a number.

"Any doubt about it?" Grice demanded.

"No," Rollison answered, shortly. He felt an unreasoning resentment at the way Grice talked, and even at Jolly, for failing to notice and warn him about this. He kept his feelings on a tight leash, however, determined not to show how raw his nerves were. They were much more sensitive than usual, and that puzzled and even worried him.

Was his touchiness due to Lola?

"You admit it's yours?" said the Winchester Superintendent, as if astonished.

"No point in denying it," said Rollison, and added sarcastically, "Will anyone object if I point out that I didn't use it?"

The Winchester man didn't speak.

"It's been wiped clean of prints," said Grice awkwardly. "And you could have done that."

"Well, I didn't."

"Maybe not," said Grice, and he smiled a little more freely. "I don't think you did, Rolly, but I think it would be possible to build a pretty strong case against you. With a little ingenuity, it might even be possible to find a motive. But I don't think any jury would convict you.

They wouldn't believe that you'd come here with our knowledge, and do this. If it weren't for that there'd be a very strong prima facie case. And of course I don't suppose the murderer realised that you'd arranged this visit with us."

"Ah," said Rollison, feeling much better. "He thought I was wearing the police uniform just to fool him. That it?"

"I should think so."

"Someone waiting in the grounds and expecting me," remarked Rollison. He took a cigarette case out of his pocket, opened it, and absentmindedly put a cigarette to his lips. He lit it, and went on: "One weakness. This chap couldn't have been sure I'd come today."

"He could be sure you'd left London, and could assume you were coming here—or at least be here in case you turned up."

"Could be," agreed Rollison. He drew the smoke deep into his lungs, and exhaled very slowly. "New angle, Bill. The idea being that I had Blacker convicted of murder, and this was a revenge in kind."

"All this talk about Blacker," the Winchester man interpolated gruffly. He was tall, florid and blond, and gave Rollison the impression that he wasn't very happy about Grice's attitude. "The man's dead and buried."

Neither Grice nor Rollison spoke.

"Well, isn't he?" demanded the Winchester man, almost angrily.

"Bill," said Rollison, shortly, "why not get an exhumation order, just to make sure?"

"I'll see about it," said Grice. Obviously, he did not reject the suggestion out of hand; probably he had been contemplating it himself. "Will you make a detailed statement before you leave? We'll have it typed, and you can sign it in the morning."

"Yes," said Rollison.

"Thanks. Now?"

"Send a message to Miss Davenport that she might have to wait for half-an-hour, will you?"

"Yes, of course," agreed Grice, and the Winchester man stirred himself and gave the order.

Rollison sat on a corner of the bed, and dictated his statement concisely to a middle-aged bald-headed sergeant whose shorthand would have qualified him for a job with Hansard. Now and again the Winchester man scowled, giving the impression that it was difficult to believe this story; but it was not until Rollison reached the visit to the New Forest Inn that Grice and the other Superintendent really began to sit up and take notice.

". . . and we came out after about an hour and twenty minutes," Rollison dictated. "A young couple was standing by the car, and afterwards went to a pale-blue motor-scooter which was parked on the other side of the car. I can give full descriptions of both girl and youth. I noticed that the lock of the car had been scratched with a metal instrument, and . . ."

When he had finished, the Winchester man said heavily:

"All right, I'm convinced. Let's have that description and we'll put out a call for the man and the girl on that motor-scooter at once. I'll see to it myself."

*   *   *

"Well, someone's after you," Grice said, in a grave voice. "And it's very well laid on."

"Yes."

"Any more ideas?"

"No," said Rollison. "Did Jolly ask you to probe into Blacker's past and find out what children he left behind?"

Grice said: "Rolly, sometimes even you forget that the police have to keep on top of their job or they wouldn't have a chance with the average crook. We have checked every one of the women with whom Blacker associated, and Divisional reports have been sent in several times.

He had a sister, but we don't know what happened to her. We are trying to find out. We've no reason to believe that he ever married; certainly he didn't under his own name, in this country. We've never traced a child by any of his mistresses. The assumption is that Blacker made sure that he couldn't be landed with a paternity order, and certainly he never was. We had one case, twenty-six years ago, of a girl found drowned after her association with Blacker. She was four months gone. But the coroner's jury returned a verdict of suicide, and at the time of the inquest we weren't really sure that Blacker had been around much with the girl. If there was a child, then it was almost certainly by a woman who didn't let Blacker know about it."

Rollison said: "Hmm. Pity."

"We can still try to check back," went on Grice, "but something new will have to turn up before it will help us. You'd like to think the killer was a son of Blacker, wouldn't you?"

"I don't mind what I think. I simply know that it must be someone with a deep affinity with Blacker, someone with a deep personal attachment, who feels more or less as Blacker would have felt. It simply isn't reasonable to believe that anyone would do it for money. Blacker might have been able to pay someone to carry out orders during his lifetime, because the killer would be scared not to, but after his death——"

Rollison broke off.

"I'll try to fix that exhumation order," Grice declared. "It might not be easy, though."

"Anything else you want me for down here?"

"No," said Grice. "No. Have you any idea what this Davenport woman really meant to Blacker?"

"He is reported to have behaved like a dear old Grandad to her," said Rollison dryly. "No. All I know is that she was attacked in New York, and that there were the booby-traps in her room and in the car. It was her door, the passenger's door, which was fitted up," Rollison went on. "There was at least a chance that she would open the door herself, or be facing the inside of the car when it was opened. Not more than one chance in two, perhaps, but in any case the explosion might have injured her and it certainly scared her. I must say she gets over scares very quickly." He began to smile faintly. "I ought to go and see how she's getting on."

"Rolly," said Grice.

"Hm-Hmm?"

"This woman has inherited half a million pounds, and she might think it worthwhile making a fool of you to make sure she earns it. She might even be the type who would enjoy seeing you on the rack, would take a sadistic pleasure out of watching the danger gradually wear you down."

"Ah," said Rollison.

"And it wouldn't be the first time you'd been fooled by a beautiful woman."

"I hope not," said Rollison firmly. "Bill, believe me, I know that she might be in this. The attacks in New York might have been laid on simply to convince me and even you that she is in danger. She herself could have put that booby-trap in her bedroom, making an intelligent guess that I would go and get her luggage, and open a case to put her clothes inside. She could have fixed the booby-trap on the door of the car, too, when I was washing and whatnot at the pub, before lunch. Also, she could have stolen that hammer from the flat. Lola's certainly in line as a suspect." It was a relief, in a way, to bring this fact into the open.

"I'm glad you realise it," said Grice.

"But, Bill."

"Yes?"

"She couldn't have killed the Moodys."

"Obviously she isn't working on her own," said Grice. "The man who rode off from here, after sneaking that ladder away, wasn't imaginary. He probably hoped it would take you longer to get down from the attic than it did, because the police had a call to go to Sandro Manor ten minutes before your call came in. It was a man's voice, no doubt about that."

"A man working with Lola," mused Rollison. "Yes, it's possible. Thanks for giving me a clean bill. Now I must go and see Lola."

He went ahead of Grice.

Young George Hanbury was sitting at the driving seat of the Bentley Continental, and Lola was at the wheel. Their heads were very close together. What the hell made Hanbury think he had that right?

Rollison approached along the grass, so that he was not heard. When he was near enough, he saw that Lola's hand was on the steering wheel, and that Hanbury's hand was over hers, as if he really believed that she did not know how to control the direction of a car. He was talking nineteen to the dozen. Nearer still, Rollison saw that Hanbury's leg was pressed tightly against hers, and that she was shamelessly leaning against him, so that he must be acutely aware of her. His face was pink, and the way he talked suggested a considerable degree of strain. She had talked him into getting into the car, of course, but it was infernal nerve!

Hanbury was saying: ". . . easiest car in the world to drive, if you know how. I don't think anyone could argue that it isn't the *best* car in the world. Ha-ha. Now try again. Press that button in at the end of the lever for neutral—I mean, to get the gear out of neutral. Then forget the little button until you want to go into reverse. Try it."

Rollison stood on the grass for a moment, then went to the back of the car, so that he could go round the other side on gravel; that way he would be nearer Lola, too, and would not have to talk across Hanbury. Hanbury was guiding her fingers on the lever attached to the steering column, completely immersed in the task.

Rollison stepped on to the gravel—and as he did so the purring engine gave an unusual rasp of sound. He sensed the danger on the instant, and sprang away. The big car jumped backwards, wheels jolting over the grass verge, and Rollison saw the grey sides pass within a few inches of him, felt the wind, heard the front tyres crunching over the gravel. It jolted to a standstill. Someone cried out from the porch, while Rollison fetched up against the side of the house with a bump. Lola and young Hanbury were twisting round in their seats to find out what the shouting was about.

The man from the porch said roughly:

"You nearly ran Mr Rollison down!"

"Did *what*?" gasped Hanbury.

"Could easily have killed him." The man came on towards Rollison, anxiously. "Are you all right, sir?"

"Recovering from the shock," said Rollison. He had to keep a tight hold on himself, he could have flayed Hanbury—but it was not really certain that the solicitor was to blame. As he spoke, Rollison heard the car door slam. A moment later Lola came running towards him, looking terribly alarmed, eyes and lips set as if in consternation, hands stretched out to touch him. Before he could escape, she was holding him tight.

"Richard, are you all right? *Are you?* If I'd hurt you I would never have forgiven myself! *Are you all right?*" She was shouting, and staring into his eyes, while Hanbury was getting out of the car hesitantly. Rollison made himself sway, gave the impression that he would have fallen but for the woman's grasp. He let his eyes roll. Lola tightened her grip, crying: "Richard, don't do that! Oh, God, he's hurt, I know he's hurt."

"Let me see——" the policeman began.

Lola still held Rollison, as Hanbury said: "It—it can't be very serious. He——"

Lola spun round on him. Through his lashes, Rollison saw the way her lips tightened and her eyes flashed with the kind of anger she had turned on him earlier in the day.

"You goddammed fool, how do you know whether he's hurt or not? And it's your fault. You pushed my hand so that I went into reverse gear. *You tried to run him down.*"

"No, here—I—really!"

"You tried to run him down, just as I was run down in New York. That's the truth of it. You're the man to blame. You're responsible for these horrible killings. Tell the truth—*you're* the murderer!"

Grice was coming at the double, the massive Winchester Superintendent behind him. Lola let go of Rollison and took Hanbury by his wrists in her favourite grip, and shaking him to and fro, so that he appeared to be stuttering even more than he was. His eyes were rounded, his fair hair flopped up and down on his forehead, he kept trying to speak.

"I—I didn't know anything about it. I didn't change gear, you did. I—I—I tell you *she* did!" he cried to Grice and the Winchester man.

"You goddammed liar!" cried Lola. She let him go and slapped him across the face, just as she had Rollison. Someone called out: "Now, steady." George Hanbury staggered back, and Lola tried to strike him again.

Now Rollison's eyes were wide open in an effort to make sure that he missed nothing, and he saw one of the most remarkable incidents in his life. Young George Hanbury, flabbergasted at first, tightened his lips, and narrowed his eyes. In place of surprise there was anger, and anger turned to fury when Lola's nails scratched his cheek.

Instead of backing away, he leapt forward. Before any of the policemen could stop him, he had gripped Lola's wrist. Then he twisted. Lola gave a little yelp of pain, and next moment went hurtling through the air, flung bodily away from Hanbury as if by the flick of a wrist. She

kicked against a tuft of grass and went sprawling backwards, her legs waving high into the air, her skirt falling
down around her waist. Then she went right head over
heels.

"Don't you try that again, you bitch," Hanbury said in
a quivering voice.

In that moment, he looked like a killer.

14

EXHUMATION ORDER

GRICE was now between Hanbury and Lola, while the Winchester man, after the first moment of surprise, rushed to Lola's aid. A policeman holding Rollison let him go, and was practically oblivious because he was gaping at Lola. The remarkable thing was the ease with which she turned that somersault, and the speed with which she did a handspring and reached her feet. Her clothes dropped back into position. Her hair was disarrayed and her collar rucked up, but otherwise there was nothing the matter with her.

"You little bastard," she said viciously.

"Don't you call me——" Hanbury began, and tried to rush past Grice to get at the woman. Grice put out a hand to stop him, as Rollison took out the box of phials. Hanbury turned on him with the same viciousness, caught him entirely by surprise, and sent him staggering away. Now there was no one between Hanbury and Lola, and it looked as if the youth would fling himself at her.

Rollison flicked one of the glass containers, and it cracked and broke against Hanbury's glasses. A wisp of vapour appeared, followed by the faint odour of tear-gas—enough would be released to take effect before the phial fell. Hanbury began to beat at the air, and to cough and splutter. Almost at the same moment, Lola began to cough, and swung away. Grice recovered his balance, took Hanbury's right arm, thrust it upwards in a hammer lock, and marched him a dozen paces off. Then he let him go. Tears were already streaming down the youngster's face, his glasses had fallen off, and he was gasping for breath. Lola had stopped coughing, but her eyes were watering, and for the first time her beauty was really impaired.

"The stinging won't last long," Rollison said mildly.

"Are you—are you all right, sir?"

"Thanks, yes," said Rollison.

"They nearly ran you down."

"So I noticed."

Grice called: "Do you think it was deliberate, Rolly?"

"I wasn't near enough to the driving wheel to know."

"Could it have been?"

"They could have seen me in the wing mirror," Rollison answered. His quick success had smoothed away the mood of irritation. "The problem would be to be certain who did it. I'm sure that Lola——"

He saw Lola start, and move towards him, and he quite expected another outburst; instead, she stood still in front of him, the tears trickling down her face so that her make-up was ravaged even more. In a husky voice, she said:

"I didn't know you were there, I swear I didn't. Hanbury was responsible, Richard. He forced my hand down, and—and *he* pressed that button at the end of the gear lever. I swear to you that he pressed it. I didn't mean to go into reverse, I knew I was too near the grass. *He* did it, Richard."

"One person's word against another's," said the Winchester man, formally.

"We're going to call it an accident," Rollison declared. "You might have a talk with young Hanbury, Bill, and try to calm him down. You might also tell me why you called him illegitimate." Rollison looked at Lola with a forced smile. "Was that simply a term of abuse?"

She said: "Why, yes, of course it was."

"I shouldn't use it too freely," Rollison said. "It could get you into more trouble, especially if the remark happened to be associated with Blacker. Do you want to bathe your eyes?"

"They'll be all right."

"Bill," said Rollison, "do you mind if we go back to London now?"

"You go ahead, but don't drive too fast" agreed Grice. "A police car will follow you, and we don't want you out of the driver's sight. I'll see that Hanbury gets back to Town." Hanbury was still coughing, but was now trying to dry his eyes with his handkerchief. All the fight seemed to have been knocked out of him.

The Winchester man opened the door of the driving seat of the Bentley, and said:

"Very glad to have seen you in action, Mr Rollison. I'm afraid I was a bit short-tempered in the house. The truth is, it looked so cut and dried I began to think you'd got a special pull at the Yard. Nonsense, I know." He held out his hand. "Hope you'll take up residence here one of these days."

"You never know," said Rollison. He felt much better.

* * *

"Richard," said Lola, half-an-hour later.

"Yes, my sweet?"

"What did you throw at that little beast?"

"A small phial of tear-gas."

"Did you just happen to have it with you?"

Rollison, driving at a steady sixty, smiled and said: "I always like to happen to have something with me. I've known a lot of moments when I've needed it. Today's best bet was tear-gas in a fragile glass phial. Never known to fail."

"I didn't really believe that you were such a remarkable man."

"No blarney, honey-bun," murmured Rollison.

"That's not blarney, it's what I feel already." She rested her fingers on the back of his hand, not hard enough to affect the steering wheel. "How well do you know that little beast?"

"George Hanbury? I've only known him for a couple of days."

"He really meant to knock you down."

"Or he could have been too anxious to squeeze your hand," said Rollison. "Unless you saw some glint in his eyes, or heard a hissing intake of breath, or noticed the way his body tensed at the moment he hurtled the car towards me."

"Darling," said Lola very softly, "I don't think any of this is funny."

"All right, it's not funny."

"Richard," said Lola, ten miles further on, after he had been forced to concentrate on passing several heavy trucks.

"Yes, my sweet."

"Could George Hanbury be Gus Blacker's son?"

"If you mean, is his age about right, yes, I suppose he could. There's not the remotest facial or physical likeness, and I wouldn't put my money on him being the product of a beautiful woman and a handsome man, would you?"

"He's like a little monkey."

"Well, a little like a friendly monkey much of the time. He could be Blacker's son, of course, if the devil had one."

"You ought to hate him," Lola said.

"He would say that I ought to hate you."

Five miles and three middle-of-the-road crawlers ahead, Lola said:

"Do you?"

"Do I what?"

"Hate either George Hanbury or me?"

"Not yet."

"What would make you?"

Rollison said: "I wouldn't have much love or affection for anyone involved in the murder of that caretaker and his wife, or for anyone who tried to blind another human being, or burn one to death. But we're a long way from finding out who is responsible, so let's concentrate on the practical. You may have forgotten one unfortunate factor."

"Have I?"

"You have a lot of formalities to go through, and as one of the Trustees, George Hanbury can make it hard or easy."

"Oh, there's no need to worry about that," said Lola off-handedly. "If you think it's necessary, I can have him eating right out of my hand by the morning. And if it's better not to have anything to do with him, I can insist on being dealt with by the senior partner. *Is* his name Gammon?"

"Yes."

"Richard."

"Yes?"

"Why did Blacker choose the firm of Gammon and Hanbury to handle his estate and make his will?"

"I don't know."

"If George Hanbury was his son, that would explain it, wouldn't it?"

"If Gammon and Hanbury had done a good job of handling his defence, that would explain it, too. Blacker was sentenced to death for murdering a man in a fight inside a club, and should have been hanged, but the Home Secretary reprieved him. Her Majesty's pleasure turned out to be ten years. He might have been grateful to Gammon and Hanbury because of that, their presentation of the plea to the Home Secretary."

"Are you going to find out more about the reasons?"

"I'm going to try to."

"From the police?"

"They're the safest bet."

"Rolly," said Lola, very thoughtfully, "I thought you preferred to work on your own. They called you the best private eye in England."

"Bill Grice and I have been co-operating quite well together for a long time," replied Rollison, "and we get a lot of results between us. The Blacker case really began that, years ago. We don't live in each other's pockets, but we get along. Now, sweetheart, we're running into a lot of traffic. Let me concentrate on driving."

"You're not a bit like the reckless daredevil I expected you to be," said Lola, thoughtfully, and added: "I suppose it's harder to take the calculated risk, like you do."

"Let's just amuse ourselves wondering what Jolly's getting ready for supper," said Rollison, and Lola laughed and settled down in her seat. She did not speak again until they were at the end of the Great West Road, and it was beginning to get dark. Then she said unexpectedly:

"Did I shock you?"

"I take a lot of shocking."

"I can't rid myself of *everything* I learned in Brooklyn."

"A Brooklyn Babe, were you?" asked Rollison.

"It's where I spent my childhood—in the streets where they lived six in a room."

"Lola," said Rollison, "anyone who can start life in the part of Brooklyn you're talking about, and grow into what you are, has my admiration every time."

"I think that must be one of the nicest things anyone has ever said about me," declared Lola. Rollison snatched a glance at her. She looked as if she meant exactly what she said.

*   *   *

"I have a plain omelette in mind, sir," said Jolly, "and afterwards, if Miss Davenport would like it, I suggest a *soufflé.*"

"Lola?" inquired Rollison.

"It sounds like a dream."

"Plain omelette and a cheese *soufflé,*" confirmed Rollison.

"Very good, sir," said Jolly, and went towards the kitchen.

"Jolly."

"Sir?"

"Did you really fail to notice that the Blacker hammer had been taken away?"

"It was there last night, sir, and I hadn't inspected the wall this morning. I'm very much afraid that I did not observe that it was missing. Is there anything more?"

"Not now," said Rollison, expecting Lola to ask what this was all about. She was looking at him intently. He smiled to himself because her make-up was in need of repair, her hair was still disarrayed, and the smeared, dried-up tears at her eyes suggested that she had been crying. She looked at him pensively, without glancing at the empty hook on the wall; then she asked in a cooing voice:

"Will you mind if I change into a robe before supper?"

"Of course not. I'll do the same."

"And may I use one of those beautiful silk robes in the guest room?"

"They're for you to use."

"Rolly," she said pensively, "I was asking Jolly, and he informed me that you have no sisters, no young cousins, and no female relations who would find any of the clothes or the make-up accessories in that spare room right for them."

"Jolly knows everything," observed Rollison. He wished Lola hadn't raised the subject; it would have been more in character to accept the situation without comment, but his momentary flash of irritation soon subsided.

"I wish I knew everything about you," Lola remarked, and went out.

Rollison went into his room, had a quick shower, changed into royal blue pyjamas and a darker blue dressing-gown, and went back to the big room. Jolly had set table mats and knives and forks on a small table; supper style. Rollison switched on a hi-fi record player, considered, and put on some records of traditional jazz. He turned the player low, and went back to his chair. As he sat down, Lola called: "Hi, Richard," and he got up—and stopped in his tracks.

He had forgotten the exquisite dressing-gown which he had acquired some years ago for a very lovely lady. It was a soft golden colour, and fitted Lola's figure a little more tightly than it should. But the remarkable thing was that she had washed her face and not put on make-up, and had combed her hair straight back from her forehead. Any other woman would have been Plain Jane as a result; she was devastating.

"Now you've really forgiven me," she said, and squeezed his hand as he helped her into her chair . . .

Jolly's *soufflé* was exactly right.

Lola was sitting back, a hand at the arm of her chair, moving her head and her feet gently to the rhythm of the blues, her eyes half closed and their expression dreamy. Rollison sat back, smoke curling from a cigarette, brandy by his side, comfortable, almost able to forget what it was all about and why she was here.

The telephone bell rang.

He turned his head towards it, resentfully; he did not want any interruption. Lola continued to look up at the ceiling, as if oblivious. The bell kept ringing. Jolly, Rollison suspected, was having a bath. He got up slowly, with the *brr-brrr* raucous above the music, still resentful and now a little anxious. He did not want anything to break the spell.

He lifted the receiver. "Rollison."

"Rolly," said Grice, "we've got that exhumation order, and we're going to check Blacker's body now. Would you like to be there to see for yourself?"

15

NO REASONABLE DOUBT

"WELL?" asked Grice, gruffly.

"There's no reasonable doubt," said the youthful pathologist. They were in a small hall near the cemetery where Blacker had been buried: Grice, Rollison, the pathologist and two attendants. "Malformation of the left hand at the third index and little finger, due to an accident in childhood. Appendix scar and scar of an abscess which followed the appendix operation. Two scars on the right side of the breast, commensurate with stab wounds—as described on the official description in *Records*. Ridged scar behind the left ear running round towards the carotid artery—also on the official description form. Scar on the skull, as a result of a blow with a blunt instrument—yes, it's Blacker. There's no reasonable doubt."

Rollison didn't speak.

"Well, that's what we wanted to know," said Grice. "I didn't really think there was any doubt, Rolly, did you?"

"Don't hardly know what I thought," said Rollison. "Are you coming now?"

"Yes."

They said good night to the others, went out into the warm June night, which was bright with stars. It was nearly half past three, and Grice stifled a yawn.

"Where does it lead us?" he asked, through the yawn.

"To the unbelievable," said Rollison. "That someone was so devoted to Blacker that he or she would lay on this kind of campaign without hope of reward." In turn, he stifled a yawn. "Believe that?"

"I don't know what to believe," Grice said. "If Miss Davenport's money were to go to someone else if she wasn't here to enjoy it, there'd be good reason to murder her, wouldn't there?"

"Yes," agreed Rollison. "But I read the will, and she gets everything after the smaller bequests are paid. The Press hasn't dug anything new up, as far as I can find out. Jolly says there was a crowd of them at the flat for much of the day, but he managed to get rid of them by saying I wasn't coming home."

"Trust Jolly," said Grice. "Well, I'm with you this far—I can't see anyone doing this for love, and I don't see how they could be doing it for money, unless——"

"Lola Davenport's paying them," said Rollison.

"Could it be a condition under which she inherits?"

"Oh, come," protested Rollison. "How could such a condition be enforced? If Blacker were alive he could threaten to alter his will, but he can't alter it posthumously. I suppose there could be a later will, which someone is holding over Lola's head as a threat, but—no, that's just a fancy. If there was another will in favour of someone else, that someone would have to be pretty devoted to Blacker's memory to keep it secret and let Lola get away with the boodle."

"What's your real opinion of her?" demanded Grice.

Rollison said: "I'd like to think she was honest and quite innocent of any part in this."

"Fallen for her?"

The question irritated Rollison. "It wouldn't be difficult," he said tartly.

"Well, don't make the mistake of trusting her yet," advised Grice. "What about Hanbury?"

"A young man with a quality of viciousness I hadn't suspected," Rollison said, "but I don't know anything about him. I needn't ask you to find out where he came from, and why his firm worked for Blacker."

"Oh, I can tell you that," said Grice. "It was old

Gammon, the senior partner, who prepared Blacker's defence. He was a middle-aged articled clerk at that time, but did the job all right. He started the firm of Gammon and Hanbury a few years afterwards, with the money that Blacker gave him for saving his neck."

"Well I'm damned," said Rollison. "It looked as if it had been in that office for centuries."

"In a way it has," said Grice. "There were two other partners, very old men, when he took over. They included another Hanbury, this one's uncle. When the old men died, the firm was owned by Gammon and young Hanbury, who inherited a quarter share."

"So you've been checking already," Rollison said. "I ought to have expected it." He was annoyed with himself for not thinking about it earlier. "If Hanbury's a descendant partner, so to speak, can he be an illegitimate son of Gus Blacker?"

"I'm going to check," said Grice. "It's conceivable that he was not a nephew but adopted by old Hanbury. Can't afford to take anything for granted."

"Not a thing," agreed Rollison, solemnly. "Gammon and Hanbury don't seem very prosperous today. They don't seem to employ any staff worthwhile."

"I know," said Grice. "The one reliable is an elderly Irishwoman once a secretary, nowadays a kind of care-taker, message-taker and general factotum for years. She was pressed into service to nurse Blacker in his last illness. As a firm they did everything possible for him, much more than any firm of solicitors normally would."

"Any special reason?" inquired Rollison.

"I've no evidence of any," said Grice. "Mrs Regson has a grandson who lives at the flat above the offices with her when he's home, but that's not often. He's in the Merchant Navy. Take it from me, though, I'll check Gammon and Hanbury very closely." They were stand-ing by the side of Grice's car as they talked, and a driver was a few yards away. "Get in, I'll take you home."

"Thanks," said Rollison. He got in, leaned back in the car, and kept looking at Grice, who was not only tired but deeply preoccupied. Rollison hardly knew whether to be pleased or sorry about the result of the exhumation. He found himself trying to look at the situation so that he could see anything which the police might have missed. His one great advantage over the police was that he could take chances which they dared not. In this case, so far, he had been over-cautious. The time was coming when he would probably have to make young Hanbury talk—and he was more likely to be able to do that than the police. What hadn't he checked, or what hadn't Grice checked?

He couldn't recall anything to mind until he was half way up the stairs of the Gresham Terrace house. The light at the landing was still on, so that he could see everywhere; he hoped that Jolly had gone to bed.

He said aloud: "Ticky Mendelsohn would hold the money bags."

Ticky Mendelsohn had been Blacker's accountant.

He was thinking about Ticky, a middle-aged Jew who was well known in the East End, who was not above blinking at certain unorthodox financial activities, but whose reputation in general was sound. Ticky was really a cross between an unofficial legal adviser and an accountant, and he always liked to keep on the right side of the law. Grice hadn't mentioned him; that might mean that Grice was working on him but keeping mum about it. Rollison smiled rather sourly, then reached a turn in the stairs, and stopped abruptly. A man was leaning against the wall just outside his flat. The odd thing was that he had his back to Rollison, and was not moving. After the first moment of surprise, Rollison began to go up very softly. The man looked almost as if he were asleep standing up, and certainly didn't move. Rollison reached the landing, and was within arm's reach of the man.

Softly, he said: "Good evening."

He saw the other start, and was ready for a whirlwind attack. Instead, the man turned slowly, keeping his back to the wall. Defensively? His eyes were bleary, as if he had in fact been dozing.

"So you made it," he muttered. "Thought Jolly was a lying son-of-a-gun, and you were in all the time. I'm from the *Record*. Mind answering a few questions, Mr Rollison?"

Keeping his patience, Rollison answered those questions he wanted to, and evaded those he preferred not to answer. He agreed that Lola Davenport had been staying with him as his guest. The young man went off, shoulders squared, manner perky now, and wide awake. Rollison let himself in.

Nothing in the flat suggested that there had been trouble. The big room had been tidied before Jolly had gone to bed. Rollison yawned as a church clock not far off struck four. He paused outside Lola's door, hesitated, and went past. It would not have surprised him had he found her in his room, but she wasn't. The bed was turned down, as usual, the window was open a few inches; in fact everything was normal. He undressed quickly, and the bed seemed to invite him. He flung back the bedclothes as he stood on one foot by the side of the bed, to get in.

There was a muffled roar; a flash; a tongue of flame from the bottom of the bed itself.

* * *

"That would have done a lot of damage if I'd gone in feet first," Rollison said. "When did you make the bed, Jolly?"

"This morning, just after breakfast, sir. As usual," Jolly said. He was standing in his dressing-gown, and with a plastic fire extinguisher in his hand. Rollison held another. The window was wide open, but the stench remained and every now and again Rollison coughed.

"So it was made when young Hanbury called here today, you say."

"Yes, sir."

"Could he have done this?"

"There was a moment when he was on the way out, and I was at the back door talking to a tradesman, sir. If Hanbury knew exactly what he was planning, he would have time to slip the contraption down into the bed, but when I came to turn the bed down, this evening, I saw no indication that the bedclothes had been disturbed."

"So—who?"

With great care, Jolly said: "Miss Davenport has had ample opportunity, sir, and the contraption is very small and could easly be concealed in a handbag, possibly in a purse."

"Yes, I know. Anyone else?"

Jolly said: "I've been in practically all day. The Wrightsons were here when I was at Fortnum and Masons, and shopping in Shepherd Market. There have been a number of newspapermen in and out all day, as I told you, and occasionally I left several of them together while I dealt with urgent matters. Any one of them could have gone into that bedroom, but I wouldn't have thought it likely."

"Did you check each one?"

"Most of them I recognised, but a few were unfamiliar, and I asked to see their credentials."

"Did they have them?"

"Yes, sir."

"Hmm," said Rollison. "Jolly."

"Sir?"

"How deeply must you sleep not to hear that explosion just now?"

"*Very* deeply indeed," said Jolly.

"So deeply that if that didn't disturb you, you would still be very fast asleep."

"Indubitably, sir."

"Get the master key," ordered Rollison, "and stand by to check that I'm not making a fool of myself, will you? If she so much as flickers an eyelid we'll turn ourselves into a modern inquisition. You ready for the job?"

"I will be very glad to co-operate," said Jolly.

Rollison waited for a few minutes while Jolly went for the key. He felt wide awake, and much more alert than he had when he had been with Grice and the pathologist. There were no sounds except the faint ones made by Jolly's movement. He saw Jolly coming back, key in hand; it was better to use the key than a picklock, because the key could be handled without any noise. Jolly had oiled it. Rollison slid it into the lock and turned slowly and carefully, but it had nothing to turn, and there was no key in the other side. When he withdrew the key and turned the handle, the door yielded.

"It didn't exactly scare her out of her wits," Rollison whispered. He pushed the door a few inches, and they stood listening.

After a few seconds, the soft sound of Lola's breathing was audible, very soft, very regular. Rollison pushed the door wider open. The light from a street lamp showed at the window and on the ceiling but Lola's face and head were in shadows. He could only just discern them. She didn't move. He shone a torch towards the ceiling, so that no sudden light would shine on her, and perhaps disturb her. She was sleeping on her side, head down and cradled on her arm, a little uncomfortably; not a wholly natural pose, yet not one which anyone was likely to assume, being too difficult to maintain. Rollison could just see the movement at her lips. Her left shoulder was bare, and the tips of her fingers showed just above the sheet.

Gradually Rollison lowered the torch so that it shone on the pillow, and was very bright near her face. She did not stir, and her eyelids did not flicker. Her lips were parted, and she seemed to be breathing through her mouth—but very, very softly. Jolly moved round so that he could see her more clearly, and then Rollison shone the torch straight into her face.

She still did not stir.

If she were pretending, could she keep her eyelids so still? Wasn't some little twitch inevitable? As he stared at her, Rollison tried to make himself believe that she was really asleep, that she hadn't heard the explosion. He began to frown.

Jolly whispered: "She *is* asleep, sir."

Rollison said: "Yes. Take the torch, Jolly." He put it into his man's hand. "Shine it straight on to her face." Jolly kept the torch very steady. It shone upon that exotic beauty—and it seemed to Rollison that he was indeed looking upon the face of a child.

He said in a quiet voice: "Lola."

She didn't stir.

"Lola," he said, and put out a hand and touched her shoulder; her flesh was warm. He raised his voice "*Lola!*"

She didn't show any sign of movement. He gripped the top of her arm tightly, and shook her; and as he did so he felt a kind of panic, a suffocating panic different from anything he had known before. He kept shaking. "*Lola wake up!*"

She lay there like a child.

"For God's sake——"

"I don't think there is anything to worry about, sir," said Jolly, and his voice was reassuringly cool. "I should say that she took some kind of sleeping draught."

"Or was given one," Rollison said roughly, and now he put both hands on her shoulders, turned her on her back and shook her vigorously. "Lola, wake up. Do you hear me? Wake up!"

Her head jolted to and fro.

16

STILL THE BEAUTY SLEEPS

"Jolly," said Rollison, tautly.

"Yes, sir?"

"Try her pulse."

"Very good, sir," Jolly said. "But I feel sure there is nothing to worry about, she——"

"Just try her pulse," Rollison repeated harshly.

Jolly inclined his head, and his forefinger sought Lola's wrist. Rollison watched his man's rather browned, wrinkled finger against the smoothness of Lola's flesh. He felt suffocated, and tried to tell himself that he was a fool, that this woman didn't mean anything to him, certainly no more than a passing *affaire*; yet, in some compelling way, she did mean more.

He was tired, of course. It had been a tricky day, and there had been the booby-trap in his bed, enough to shock any man; he wasn't himself. But he knew that these were excuses. He was worked up because of the possibility that Lola was not just sleeping from some mild drug. She was the obvious suspect, she could have committed all the crimes today except the murder of the caretaker and his wife, but she mattered to him.

Jolly said: "It is a little fainter than one might expect, but quite steady."

"Yes," said Rollison. "Eyes."

Jolly placed his right hand above the sleeping woman's eye, rested the fingers on her forehead, placed the thumb firmly on the eyelid, and raised it. It was strange to see Lola like that. Rollison bent nearer.

"Pin-point pupil," he remarked. "Morphine."

"One of the opiates, sir."

"The question is, how much?" said Rollison. "Ought we to send for a doctor?"

He knew that Jolly was looking at him a little strangely.

"I really don't think it necessary, sir—a drug of this kind would take some time to take effect, and I think that if the dose had been really heavy, Miss Davenport would have been in a different kind of sleep—a coma, sir. I really think that she will be all right if we leave her. But if you would feel happier if we had a doctor——" Jolly broke off.

He was right, of course, there could be no reasonable argument about that, and yet there remained an edge of doubt, and Rollison did not feel that he could take risks. He did exactly the same as Jolly had already done. That rather faint pulse might get worse. Jolly might be over-optimistic.

"Ring Dr Welling, Jolly."

"Very good, sir."

"Think I'm making a damned fool of myself?"

Jolly said: "I'll ring at once." By his evasion, he had really answered: "Yes." He went out of the guest room, and Rollison put on the ceiling light. It was subdued; the best light in here was one over the dressing-table. This showed this woman in all her simple beauty, and he felt his heart beating faster, almost suffocating him again. He felt the perspiration on his forehead, and the dryness of the roof of his mouth. He began to look round the room, trying to think of any place where another booby-trap might be set—and as he did these things, and as he urged Jolly to hurry, the other half of his mind told him that he was making an utter fool of himself. Lola could have put that booby-trap there, could be responsible for all the booby-traps. If she was, she might have drugged herself to make it impossible for them to question her.

He would talk to her just as soon as he could.

Jolly came back. "Dr Welling will be here in a few minutes," he reported.

"Good." Rollison moved towards the door. "Now I think I need a drink."

Jolly followed him out of the room, and asked as they reached the big room:

"What happened at the exhumation, sir?"

"Blacker's dead all right."

"Ah," said Jolly.

"What does that cryptic comment mean?" demanded Rollison. He poured himself out a whisky, splashed in a little soda, and offered the bottle to Jolly. Jolly helped himself, sparingly. Rollison found it difficult not to raise his voice. "Well, what does it mean?"

"Nothing in particular, sir, but——"

"Don't lie to me, Jolly."

Jolly said: "That wasn't my intention, sir," very quietly.

"I asked you if you thought I was making a damned fool of myself."

"And I evaded that question because it isn't possible to answer it objectively in a few words," said Jolly. "May I be very frank?"

"You don't usually hesitate," Rollison said. He was being far more sharp-tempered than the circumstances warranted. He simply couldn't help it. "Let's have it."

"I think that the situation is developing exactly as Blacker would want it if he were alive, sir. From the beginning, it has been a deliberate, and if I may say so, a very clever and concentrated attempt to unnerve you. Unnerve isn't quite the right word, but——"

Rollison said stiffly: "It will do."

"And the pressure of events is so great that it is difficult for you to recover from one form of shock before another confronts you," said Jolly. "With a strange kind of irony, even Mr Grice makes the situation worse. It is most unusual for him or for the police to call you at the late hour that Mr Grice did, and the experience of going to the exhumation, the very fact that doubt about the identity of the corpse has been in your mind, all added to the strain."

Rollison said: "I'm not usually affected by strains and stresses."

Jolly didn't speak; in the ensuing silence, there was the sound of footsteps outside. Jolly moved so that he could see in the periscope mirror and murmured: "It is Dr Welling, sir," and went to admit the middle-aged doctor.

*   *   *

"Morphine, I would say, and she'll probably be un-conscious all tomorrow morning. She might even stay under most of tomorrow," Welling said. "When she comes round she'll be a bit drowsy, and will probably think she's just had a little nap. There's nothing to worry about at all. Keep her warm, and when she comes round, give her some sweet coffee. Dammit, Rolly, you know the drill. Surprised you were worried about her. Making sure you didn't set the Yard by the ears, eh?"

"That's it," said Rollison.

*   *   *

He lay in bed, dozing. It was already daylight, and the morning was so warm that he needed only a sheet over him. The stink of the fire-extinguisher foam had almost gone. Blankets had been folded over the damaged foot of the bed, and there was no other damage except to the bed and the bedclothes. He told himself that he would have to be very careful indeed. Whether there was any sense in it or not, he was much more on edge than he ought to be. Jolly was absolutely right. The truth was, of course, that he had been working at pressure for some time past, and it was emergencies of this kind which caught one on the wrong foot.

He could not make up his mind what to think about Lola, but he knew one thing for certain: if Blacker were alive he could not plan this campaign more skilfully; even the timing was perfect.

The great difficulty confronting Rollison was that of assessing his opponent, sizing him up, and anticipating the next move. Had Blacker been alive, it would have been comparatively easy; now, he was fighting someone trained by Blacker.

Ah!

He smiled wryly at the way he had picked Jolly up for saying 'ah'. Well, what did the word 'trained' amount to? For the first time he had put into words the obvious fact: that someone trained by Blacker was making this series of attacks. Could Lola have been 'trained' by Blacker? He had seen her every year for at least five years, and she had a very quick mind. But even if she were Blacker's own child, could he have filled her with the kind of vindictive hatred that was motivating this campaign?

Rollison kept coming back to the same thing: first, that someone who benefited from carrying out his orders must be involved; and second, now more clearly apparent, that it was someone who had been trained by Blacker.

Who would benefit?

He ran through the names of people, including anyone who had worked for Blacker and who might be paid by, say, Ticky Mendelsohn. Then his thoughts began to blur, and for the first time his eyes closed almost without him realising it . . .

He woke, to broad daylight and everyday sounds. He lay on his back, staring at the ceiling. Outside, the sky was a vivid blue, but there was something different from the usual morning light. He realised that with half his mind, while recollection of what had happened filled the rest. Lola; how was she? Hanbury; had the police discovered anything more about him?

Rollison hitched himself up in bed, and stared at the window. What *was* different? He scowled. It shouldn't be important, and yet in a way it was. One thing dawned on him; he had woken of his own accord, Jolly hadn't called him. Well, Jolly did occasionally let him lie in. What time was it?

Ah!

The shadows cast by the chimneys on the roofs on the street behind Gresham Terrace; that was the difference. These were being thrown towards Rollison, which meant that the sun was shining from the west. It must be late afternoon. He raised his voice: "*Jolly!*" sat further up in bed, leaned over, and pressed the bell push. He scowled at the door, yet warned himself that he must not take it out on Jolly, who must have let him sleep on deliberately. Why the devil didn't he come? There were footsteps outside, and then the door opened and a little, thin, rather wizened man appeared: this was Percy Wrightson, one of Ebbutt's men who often stood in for Jolly.

"Arternoon, Mr Ar!" Wrightson greeted with a breezy heartiness which was the last thing Rollison wanted at this juncture. "Got yer sleep up, 'ave yer? 'Ow abouta cuppa char?"

Anything to get him out of the room.

"Please. Where's Jolly?"

"Just the thing, a nice cuppa char," said Wrightson brightly, and then clapped his hands and swung round, as if on parade. He began to whistle. Rollison stared at the open door. Had Wrightson deliberately evaded that question about Jolly? What time *was* it? Was there any reason to think that anything else had gone wrong? The normal assumption that Jolly had gone out shopping, leaving Percy to take over, wouldn't apply at this time of day. Rollison looked at the clock at his side. It had stopped fairly early in the morning, at half past six; Jolly had either stopped it, or forgotten to wind it up the previous day. Rollison saw his clothes draped over the back of a chair, as he had left them last night, and sight of them made one thing almost certain: Jolly hadn't been in here this morning or he would have taken those clothes for pressing. Rollison hitched himself further forward, clutched the coat, and pulled it towards him. The chair nearly fell. He saved it, groped for his watch, took it out and looked at the face.

Half past *six*.

He had slept for twelve hours.

Lola?

He pushed back the bedclothes, grabbed his dressing-gown, and wrapped it round him as he went into the passage, and into the guest room.

The bed was made. There was no sign of Lola, except the oddments on the dressing-table. Rollison felt the rising of panic again, and fought it down. What the hell was the matter with him?

He heard the rattle of crockery as Wrightson came out of the kitchen, carrying a tray. He stopped at sight of Rollison, and said:

"Now, naughty naughty, you ought to be——"

"Stop that bloody nonsense and tell me where everyone is," rasped Rollison.

He knew that Wrightson had probably never heard him speak like that, and had doubted whether he was capable of it. Wrightson gaped, as he would have gaped at Lola. Then he moistened his lips, and said: "Yessir." He made a great play of standing aside for Rollison to go into his room. He followed, and put the tray down. "Tea as requested, sir."

Rollison said: "Percy, I've got a head that kicks like a horse."

"How about a couple of aspirins, sir?"

The offence had gone deep, or it would not be 'sir' but 'Mr Ar'.

"Later," said Rollison. "Where's Jolly?" He did not want to ask Wrightson about Lola; the way in which Lola affected him was something he preferred to keep entirely to himself. Wrightson was pouring milk into a cup, and

Rollison opened his mouth to snap at him, stopped himself in time, waited until Wrightson was handing him the tea, and then repeated:

"Where's Jolly?"

Wrightson said: "The truth is, Mr Ar, we dunno."

Rollison stared, with the cup half way to his lips. The 'Mr Ar' had helped momentarily, but all thought of that faded as he tried to absorb the implications of the answer. A question sprang to his lips angrily; he choked it back.

"Who do you mean by 'we', Percy?"

"Me'n Bill Ebbutt and Gricey," declared Wrightson, with the air of a man who was about to plunge into deep water. "Jolly went out to do some shopping this morning, about ar'past eleven. You know 'ow 'e insists on getting the freshest veg possible, doncher? Well, 'e never come back. By one o'clock I was a bit worried, so I told Bill Ebbutt. Bill come over, and we tried to wake you but it was 'opeless, so he rang the Yard. Gricey come over, and—well, there's a call out for Jolly now, Mr Ar. They'll soon find 'im."

No one had ever spoken with less conviction.

17

HARD FACTS

ROLLISON listened to Grice on the telephone.

". . . we've a London and Home Counties call out for Jolly, but nothing's come in yet. The moment it does, I'll tell you. Ebbutt has two men at the back and front of your place, and I have two in both places, as well. We're very anxious that you shouldn't go out alone, Rolly—we don't like the way this is working one little bit."

Rollison said: "It's not exactly commending itself to me. Do you know where Miss Davenport is?"

"She spent the afternoon at Gammon and Hanbury's office," said Grice, "and the last report I had was that she was with young Hanbury at the Savoy Bar."

Rollison remembered Lola saying that she would be able to twist Hanbury round her little finger.

"And you're looking after her," said Rollison.

"Yes."

"Anything else in?" Rollison knew that he was more brusque than usual, but somehow he could not help himself.

"We have picked up one or two things," answered Grice, patiently. "The motor-scooter which was at Sandro Manor yesterday morning was almost certainly the one outside the New Forest inn. An AA Scout saw the rider pick up a pillion passenger not far from the Manor, and later saw the couple outside the inn. The rider almost certainly put that booby-trap in the Bentley."

For the first time that morning, Rollison's spirits rose.

"Not Lola?"

"Not necessarily Miss Davenport. We got some finger-prints off the door of the Bentley which coincide with some which closer examination showed on the ladder—not yours, not of anyone on record. Not young Hanbury's, either."

Rollison said: "The man Blacker trained."

"Trained?"

"Can you think of a better idea?"

"No," admitted Grice, thoughtfully. "I hadn't thought of it that way, but I see what you mean. A protégé."

"Now being paid by someone who had been paid by Blacker to see this job through."

"Yes," said Grice. Obviously he wasn't wholly convinced, and Rollison felt another surge of annoyance which he repressed; he had to keep reminding himself that it would get him nowhere to lose his temper. Why *was* he losing it so easily? Lola? He'd known beautiful women before, and at the time thought their beauty unsurpassable, but he certainly hadn't been put into this kind of anxiety-complex about them.

It was not only Lola, it was a combination of the circumstances, of course. Even that explanation didn't really convince him. *Was he frightened?* Was this striking from the grave affecting him because it was so eerie? *Mackarber.*

"Yes, trained and paid by Blacker," Grice was saying, "but surely with some personal motivation for wanting to get back at you. Take that personal reason away, and——"

Grice broke off.

Rollison said, very softly, very tensely: "Bill, Blacker wasn't the only man to hate my guts. There are plenty about, and——"

"Every man known to have a reason for hating you is being checked," said Grice.

Rollison said: "Not missing a trick, are you?"

"Want me to?"

"No," said Rollison gruffly. "I wish——" he broke off. "Any reason to believe that Jolly's been hurt?"

"The last we know, he was in Shepherd Market, buying

garden peas, new potatoes and strawberries. He was seen by one of our policewomen. He had the goods in his usual shopping bag, paid for them, and went off towards Piccadilly—also as usual. He helped an old lady with her bag, near Clarges Street, and our girl didn't see him after that. We've made inquiries but no one admits seeing him get into a taxi, or speak to another soul."

Rollison said: "Is it true you came here and tried to wake me?"

"Yes. You'd been given a dose of morphia in a drink. Miss Davenport phoned and told me you were unconscious, and I sent a doctor. He said you probably wouldn't wake up until nine or ten o'clock." There was a ghost of a chuckle in Grice's voice: "Trust you to start making a nuisance of yourself at seven in the evening."

"If you call this making a nuisance of myself——" began Rollison, angrily, then pulled himself up. After a long pause, he said: "Yes, trust me. Did you talk to Miss Davenport?"

"She seemed really worried when I arrived. She had a light lunch at the flat, and was at Gammon and Hanbury's office about a quarter to three. She's been with Gammon and Hanbury, or young Hanbury, ever since. She was in a perfect position to drug you, of course."

"Yes," said Rollison, gruffly. "Yes, I know. All right, Bill. Thanks."

"Rolly?"

"Yes?"

"I've given my men strict orders not to allow you to go out of Gresham Terrace unaccompanied. I don't want to use it, but I've a warrant for your arrest for complicity in the murder of the caretaker, Moody, and his wife. Rather than let you roam London on your own I'll use the warrant and hold you in Cannon Row."

Rollison felt a flare of anger so fierce that he did not trust himself to speak. He banged the receiver down, and pushed his chair back from the desk. His head brushed the hangman's rope. He tightened his lips as he glared at the window, angry with himself and with Grice. Some warning instinct in him was asking: 'What the hell's the matter with you? She can't mean so much as this'. And there was Jolly: he was so busy losing his temper with Grice that he hardly gave Jolly a thought. *Jolly*. Servant and friend for twenty-five years and more. Rollison was still glaring out of the window when Percy Wrightson came in, obviously timidly, and asked:

"Feeling peckish yet?"

Rollison said: "No. I—oh, is there some cold meat?"

"Nice bit've 'am," said Wrightson. "Like a little salad with it?"

"Good idea," grunted Rollison, and Wrightson turned round and crept off on tiptoe.

Rollison stood up, went along to his bathroom and had a shower, put on a pair of grey flannels and a sports jacket, saw that Wrightson was still preparing the salad, and went into Lola's room. He searched the dressing-table, the wardrobe, every corner, every place where she might be hiding a booby-trap bomb, or a drug, but he found nothing at all. There was further evidence that she was extremely tidy; everything she had of her own, and everything she had borrowed from the room, had been put neatly away. By the time he had finished, the meal was on the table, and Wrightson had exerted himself to lay it just as Jolly would have done. In better humour, Rollison began to eat.

He was half-way through the meal when he realised fully for the first time that *Jolly* was missing. Jolly might be in acute danger, and here he was, sitting down as if nothing had happened, and eating like a ghoul. He pushed the plate away, and stood up. Wrightson was coming in.

"Anything wrong wiv it, Mr Ar?"

Rollison swung round on him, glaring, and so startled Wrightson that the man stood gaping, hands at his side.

For a moment they stared at each other; then Wrightson gave a comical little salute, and turned away. His bewilderment was so obvious that Rollison knew that he ought to be amused, yet he had never felt less like laughing. What the hell was the matter with him? He'd been worked up before, he'd been anxious before, but it had never got on top of him like this. The harsh and ugly fact was that since he had been with Lola Davenport, his nerve had cracked.

No, it had begun earlier; he remembered how angry he had been with Jolly, the way he had snapped at his man, about Algoa Prendergast; so it had happened earlier than that. He felt a wave of relief again, and then began to reason that he had started to feel edgy after first seeing George Hanbury—after hearing about Blacker's will. And he could say what he liked, it was *not* because of the way this campaign seemed to be run by a dead man. He wasn't as sensitive as that; even in the past twenty-four hours he had considered the possibility quite rationally, and it hadn't really affected him.

But this mood of unreasoning temper had followed the news of the will, of course; that needed remembering. He had been perfectly normal in behaviour until he had talked to young Hanbury.

He tried to think over everything that had happened from the time the young solicitor had come breezing along the passage, and he remembered Hanbury handing him the cream, to pour into coffee in the fragile looking pale blue cups. Coffee, sugar, milk. He moved across the big room and lifted the telephone—and before he dialled, he heard Bill Ebbutt's voice.

". . . ain't like 'im a bit."

"You can say that again," declared Wrightson, who must have put this call in from Jolly's extension, for the bell certainly hadn't rung. "Bit my 'ead off free or four times, Bill. Never known 'im like it. Can't be that bit of stuff, can it?"

"He's worried about Jolly, that's what it is," Ebbutt said. "You stick close to him, Percy. I'll come over arter ten. I can't come until the pub's closed unless it's an emergency. Let me know, and never mind what Lil says if you get her on the phone first."

"Okydoke," said Wrightson. "'Ave you 'eard from Gricey lately?"

"No."

"I was 'oping you'd 'ave some news of Jolly," Wrightson said. "Proper upset me if anyfink 'appened to 'im, it would."

"Upset *you*," said Ebbutt, witheringly. "It would break the Toff's blinkin' 'eart."

Ebbutt rang off, as if he couldn't trust himself to say anything else. More slowly, Wrightson replaced his receiver. Rollison kept his in his hand while he stared at the Trophy Wall. His lips were twitching, and slowly he broke into a smile. He felt as if he had been in a cooling wind on a hot day, and was calmer in spirit than he had been for a long time. At last, he put the receiver down, lifted it again, and dialled.

Doctor Welling answered.

"Oh, hallo, Rolly. That guest of yours is all right, isn't she?"

"Your diagnosis was perfect," Rollison declared. "Try again on me, will you?"

"Want me to come over? If so, make it in half-an-hour, and——"

"Let's have a go at diagnosis by telephone," said Rollison. "Symptoms—ready?"

"Try me."

"Symptoms, then—sudden overwhelming fits of bad temper, without justification. Fly off the handle at the slightest provocation. Get mad at old friends like Grice, Jolly and Bill Ebbutt. Could be overtired, but——"

"Just confine yourself to the details, not the explanations," said Welling briskly. "Anything else?"

"A kind of savage mood, which could be caused by the case I'm working on, but no job has ever affected me like this before."

"Eating well?"

"Better than usual."

"Headaches?"

Rollison said: "I suppose there's a bit of tightness at the forehead and behind the eyes, but I wouldn't say that I have many headaches."

"Feeling easily tired?"

"Well, yes, but I've had a lot of lost sleep, if I can put it that way."

"When did all this start?"

"To be noticeable, two days ago."

"Now be more precise about this," said Welling. "I want to get it right. You say this began two days ago. Was it two plus a few hours or minus a few?"

"The afternoon of the day before yesterday."

"Did you notice any signs of it before then?"

"No. I think I was my usual sunny self."

"Were you conscious of any outbursts of temper, fits of unreasonable irritation, moods of anxiety or impatience before then?"

Rollison said: "No. What's in your mind?"

"Listen to me, Rolly, and don't fly off the handle," said Dr Welling. He paused, as if giving Rollison time to digest that. "I think you may be suffering from a form of poisoning. Poisoning is too strong a word in some ways, it isn't a poison in the lethal sense—it's a comparatively mild drug which is difficult to obtain here. It's rather like the sulpha drugs—it plays on the nerves, but in exactly the reverse way to the tranquillising drugs. They take the anxieties away and soothe the nerves. This stuff makes you bad-tempered and apprehensive. It's not habit-forming, but it takes effect quickly. I can't be sure you're suffering from it, of course, I'd need to take a blood test to make sure, but it seems to measure up, and Grice——"

"Grice!" roared Rollison.

Dr Welling said: "I knew I'd let it out sooner or later. Yes, he was talking to me this afternoon, asking me if I'd noticed anything different about you. He said that you'd been much sharper-tempered than usual. And listen, he did it to help you. He didn't——"

"All right, all right," said Rollison gruffly. "I am now under iron self-control. How do I throw off the effects, if that stuff is causing the trouble?"

"You rest for forty-eight hours, you avoid alcohol, which will give you very severe headaches, and you don't take any more of the drug."

"I see," said Rollison, heavily. "Rest."

"Yes."

"Did Grice happen to tell you that Jolly's been missing since midday?"

"He didn't tell me, but I'd heard there was a search for Jolly," said the doctor. "And I know that your impulse is to rush out and search for him. Well, don't. Just as this drug will affect your temper and mood, so it will affect your judgement. You could run into serious trouble, and not get yourself out of it. What I'd like you to do is stay there until I come over. I'll take a specimen of your blood and confirm the diagnosis in a few hours. Will you do that?"

"Yes," answered Rollison, heavily. "Yes, I'd better. Thanks." He rang off, still short-tempered and with no time for the courtesies, and glared straight into the fire-place. He was sitting there when he heard the front door bell ring, and that reminded him vividly of Jolly. Jolly would normally go into the lounge hall, look up at the periscope mirror, and report who it was. Wrightson probably——

Wrightson, soft-footed, appeared in the door leading from the lounge hall.

"Mr Ar."

"What is it?"

"It's Miss Davenport, with a curly-headed cove who looks a bit like a monkey," answered Wrightson.

"Oh," said Rollison. "Yes. Let them in, will you?" He stood up as Wrightson moved towards the front door, and he reminded himself that Wrightson had learned about the mirror and the customs of the flat from Jolly.

He kept seeing Jolly in his mind's eye.

But that wasn't the only thing which preoccupied him. He heard Lola's voice, light-hearted and almost gay; he heard Hanbury say something in a voice which made it fairly obvious that Lola had won him round. And he reminded himself that his 'mood' had started from the time of the interview with Hanbury, and that if he had taken the drug with that coffee, Hanbury couldn't have given him any more.

But Lola could.

18

POINTER?

ROLLISON steeled himself to receive them pleasantly. The tone of Lola's voice angered him. It was as if she were deliberately making light of the fact that Jolly was missing, but that was nonsense; she probably didn't know that he had not come home. When she came into the room, irritation and anger vanished. It was pointless to wonder where she had got it from, but she had on a new dress, a blue one with bold flower designs on it; a dress which looked as if it had been made from a patch torn out of the sky. It seemed to give her eyes an added brightness, and touch her beauty with the serenity of a spring day. Behind her, young Hanbury looked absurd; in fact he did look rather like a monkey—a monkey on a chain.

Lola said: "Rolly!" She came hurrying towards him, but this time both hands weren't outstretched so far, and she did not give the impression that she was setting out to captivate him. Their hands touched. "What is it?"

"Do I look as bad as that?"

"You look terrible. I thought the long sleep would do you good."

"Wrong kind of sleep," said Rollison. He glanced at Hanbury. "Hallo."

"Good—good evening, Mr Rollison. I hope I'm not intruding."

"I asked George to come here because he has something to tell us which might be very useful," Lola declared. "But Richard, what *is* the matter with you?"

Rollison forced a smile. "One thick headache worse than the worst of the morning afters," he replied. "And one worry."

"Worry? Richard, you should not have worried about me, you had no need."

He felt another flare of anger, and fought it back.

"Not about you."

"I just don't understand."

"Jolly's been missing since lunch-time."

"Jolly?" she echoed, as if stupidly. "Missing? I still don't understand you. He went out to do the shopping."

"He didn't come back."

"Oh, no," said Lola, and her grip on his hands became very tight. "I can't believe anything bad has happened to Jolly. It just isn't possible." She sounded genuinely perturbed. "Have you told the police?"

"They know."

"Then how about these friends of yours, these men outside? Didn't they do anything."

"They were looking after me."

"Oh, I see," said Lola, and she released his hands. "I can't believe that Jolly won't come back." She gave a strained laugh. "He always seemed to me the one man who would never die. Does that make sense to you?"

"It makes sense," said Rollison, and marvelled that she seemed to see so many things exactly as they appeared to him. He waved to a chair and went across to the corner cupboard which served as a cocktail cabinet.

"What will you have to drink?"

"Nothing right now, Richard," Lola said, and looked at Hanbury. "You've had quite enough for this evening, George, haven't you?"

George.

"I have indeed," said Hanbury, and he moistened his lips. "Er—Mr Rollison, I'm extremely sorry if you are the victim of some kind of domestic anxiety. I really am. I can imagine only too vividly what the disappearance of an old family retainer can mean." He ran on and on tonelessly, and Rollison would have liked to kick him. Lola seemed to sense that, and interrupted.

"George!"

Hanbury started. "Yes, Lola?"

"I don't think we ought to harass Mr Rollison for too long tonight. Why don't you tell him what you told me, and then leave him to think it over?"

"Why, yes," said Hanbury. "Yes, of course. Er—Mr Rollison, Miss Dav—I mean Lola—I mean—well, she told me why she was so angry with me yesterday, and what has been happening since she arrived in England. When I put the car into the wrong gear, by mistake, it *must* have seemed intentional. The—the general situation is hard to believe, of course, very hard, and yet—well, no wonder she was mad at me—I've got eyes. I saw the police at Sandro Manor yesterday, and—well, the Moodys *were* murdered. I did wonder whether you——"

"George," interpolated Lola in a warning voice.

"Yes, of course, silly of me," said Hanbury. "What I mean to say is, Mr Rollison, there was a business associate of Mr Blacker—an old friend—who did voice his dislike of you on a number of occasions."

Rollison said: "Who?"

"Well, he——"

"Who was it?"

Hanbury said miserably: "I am only too well aware of the risk of slander that such a statement might involve, but the truth is that his accountant, a Mr Mendelsohn, spoke of you in the most hostile way from time to time. I myself heard this on several occasions. Mrs Regson, the general factotum at our offices, overheard much more, when he was talking to Mr Blacker a few years ago. It was in the office, when they were waiting to see my partner. I understand that it was because of some activity of yours that Mendelsohn lost a very considerable sum of money. He referred to you as the Toff, and—ah—in other rather less civil terms. And it is a fact, a positive fact, that Blacker and Mendelsohn appeared to be hatching some kind of—ah—plot to have their revenge. Mrs

Regson was most distressed. At the time——" Hanbury gulped, broke off, and looked more like a helpless mummy than ever.

"Revenge," supplied Rollison, quietly; strangely enough, he felt calmer, as if the mood of anger and resentment had run itself down. "What kind of revenge?"

"Well, as a matter of fact, Mrs Regson has told me that they used the words 'make him pay' and 'own back'," answered Hanbury. "I thought they were discussing some kind of counter-action for a business reverse. It didn't occur to me that anything like this, anything involving murder, could possibly be in their minds. But in the light of what I now know, I feel it my duty to acquaint you with these facts, even at the cost of betraying a client's confidence. This Mendelsohn——"

"I know Ticky," said Rollison.

"I—I imagine that you do."

"Richard," said Lola, "you just have to tell the police about this. George doesn't want to, he wants to keep right out of trouble, but I think you ought to tell the police *and* inform them where you got the information."

"Lola!" exclaimed Hanbury.

"George, honey," she said, "you forget that I'm in danger, as well as Jolly and Mr Rollison. I don't want to lie or be disfigured, and that could easily happen to me."

"But you said that you would persuade Mr Rollison *not* to tell the police!"

"All right, Hanbury," said Rollison, brusquely. "I won't tell them yet." He saw Lola's mouth open, as if she were about to protest, and saw the relief pass over Hanbury's face. "I think there are better ways of dealing with Mendelsohn." Lola's lips began to curve, as if at last she understood what he was thinking of doing. "Who else knows about this?"

"No one!"

"What about your partner?"

"Mr Gammon knows nothing at all about it," insisted Hanbury.

"Did anyone else overhear this conversation?"

"Not to my knowledge."

"What about the rest of the staff?"

"We have a very small staff, one of whom was away ill and an elderly clerk who was always a little deaf," said Hanbury. "That is why we still use Mrs Regson to help out on occasions for taking messages and answering the telephone. You can take it that no one else heard, Mr Rollison. What—what are you planning to do?"

"Think," said Rollison.

"B-b-but——"

"I'll tell the police only in emergency," said Rollison, still brusquely. "Is there anything else?"

"No. No, I don't think so. I've been into details with Miss Dav—with Lola—about her own inheritance. Certain formalities are necessary, and it would greatly facilitate matters if she were able to stay in this country for a few weeks. I—ah—I hope you will use any influence you may have to persuade her to do that."

"I will."

"Thank you, Mr Rollison. I——"

"Are you sure that if Miss Davenport were to die, her inheritance would go to her own next of kin, whoever that may be?"

"Yes," answered Hanbury, but he looked thoroughly miserable. "It is a very great anxiety. You see, it is a rather delicate issue, and if you would prefer——" he was looking at Lola.

She threw her head back and laughed.

"Don't let it worry you George! Richard, George thinks there is something very indecent about not knowing who your father was. Don't you, George?" Her voice changed, she aped a stage conception of a Mayfair duchess. "It isn't quate nace, you know."

"I—ah—I naturally wondered whether you would like

hese personal matters discussed in front of Mr Rollison,"
aid Hanbury, stiffly; it looked as if she had annoyed him
again. "However, as you seem to have no sense of em-
barrassment, it is as well to discuss the matter fully. Miss
Davenport does not know who her father was, and never
knew her mother. She was brought up in a very poor
neighbourhood of Brooklyn, in New York City, and is
aware only that she was born out of wedlock. If in fact
her mother had other issue, there will almost certainly be
some relation who would be legally considered her next
of kin even if she had never known them. If in fact she has
a half or full brother or sister, then the legal position is
obscure. It would certainly require a long and intricate
Court case, unless, of course, there was a will, or some
settlement was made by agreement between the parties."

Rollison asked softly: "What parties, Hanbury?"

"Any rival claimants."

"I see," said Rollison. "Well, Miss Davenport, it looks
as if we have to find out more about your parents."

"I have spent much of the afternoon discussing this
very—ah—delicate question with Miss Davenport, and
Mr Gammon has already discussed it with her," declared
Hanbury. "And it appears that she is unable to give us
the slightest assistance. Even her foster parents are dead.
She had no *known* relations or close friends. It will take a
long time, a very long time, to trace anyone who knew her
when she was a child, and there is no certainty that
success will attend our efforts."

"It will have to be tried," said Rollison. "And the
police might help."

"I have no objection at all to the police being asked to
request Police Headquarters in New York to investigate,"
said Hanbury, stiffly.

Rollison said: "Have you, Lola?"

She was frowning; not deeply, more with preoccupation
than with annoyance.

"I guess not," she said at last. "When I wouldn't talk

to you about my next of kin I was feeling embarrassed, but that didn't last long. What you're saying is that I might have a next of kin who knows about the relationship and knows he or she might have a good claim to some of my money on my death. Is that right?"

"Yes."

"Boy, oh boy, do I want you to find out if that's true!"

"If you will make the formal request of Scotland Yard, I will confirm the need to make the investigation," said Hanbury. He was stilted, apparently still annoyed with Lola. "Now if there is nothing else, I think I ought to go." He looked very straightly into Rollison's eyes, and went on: "Have I your word that you will not acquaint the police of the fact that I warned you about Mendelsohn? He is, remember, a client of mine."

"Yes," said Rollison.

"Thank you." Hanbury gave a stiff little bow, and Lola caught Rollison's eye, smiling faintly.

"You have my word about something else," Rollison said.

"Indeed?"

"You have my word that if anything happens to Jolly, whether it's done by Mendelsohn, or Miss Davenport's next of kin, or some unknown relation of Blacker's, or someone who has no connection with any of these things, I will kill Jolly's killer. With my own hands."

Rollison raised his hands a little, the fingers crooked; they looked capable too of strangling a bull.

"I can only advise you in your own interests that you should never take the law into your own hands," said Hanbury, and turned towards the door.

19

TICKY MENDELSOHN

"RICHARD," said Lola.

"Yes?"

"You looked and sounded as if you meant what you said about killing Jolly's killer."

"I meant it."

"Are you sure he's dead?"

"No," said Rollison. "No. I don't even think he is. I think that whoever has kidnapped him knows how I would feel about it, and would use Jolly to force me to do what I wouldn't normally want to do."

"Such as?"

"We won't waste time guessing," said Rollison, gruffly. "Did Hanbury give a fairly true report of what you were doing this afternoon?"

"Yes, he did," answered Lola. "He and that impossible old geezer Gammon just kept on and on. Gammon drank tea all the afternoon. And the old woman—landsakes, you would think she should stay at home, preparing for the last rites." Lola moved to Rollison, who was standing with his back to the Trophy Wall, his head aching slightly. At least he had managed to control his irritation; that was probably because he now knew what had caused it. "Richard, what are you going to do about Mendelsohn?"

Rollison put his head on one side, looked at her, and asked:

"How well do you know the Gimbel's slogan?"

"The Department store?" She was surprised. "Nobody but nobody undersells Gimbels. Is that what you mean?"

"That's it," agreed Rollison. "And nobody but nobody knows what I'm going to do about anybody."

"Are you saying that you don't trust me?"

"Lola dear, I wouldn't trust a soul in this world until I know the truth," Rollison declared. "I think that Jolly has been kidnapped so that someone can exert pressure on me—I shall be instructed to do some specific thing if I want to save Jolly's life. And it will probably be soon."

Lola said: "I think I understand." After a pause, she went on: "How far would you go?"

"Nobody but nobody knows how far I would go," insisted Rollison. "Now I must tell Grice about your early life in Brooklyn, and get him busy." He moved to the telephone.

Lola said: "I guess you know what you're doing," and went to her room.

*   *   *

"Bill," said Rollison.

"Yes."

"I want to make a trip."

"Nothing doing, Rolly."

"It's essential."

"You can stay at Gresham Terrace, or you can be picked up and lodged at Cannon Row for the night. I'll get busy on this New York end——"

"I wonder you hadn't started it before. I'm serious—— I want to make a trip."

"You can't."

"Bill," said Rollison, gripping the telephone very tightly, "you know as well as I do that at times there are things I can do a lot better than you."

"Not tonight and not tomorrow."

"You don't know what——"

"I've talked to Dr Welling again," said Grice. "He confirmed that you wouldn't have a chance if you tried anything on your own."

"He's talking out of the back of his neck."

"I don't think so. If you want anyone picked up and questioned, tell me who it is."

"You wouldn't get the right answers."

"You might be surprised."

"Bill, for the last time, will you call your watchdogs off?"

"No, I will not," said Grice. "Sorry, Rolly. You're not a fit man. I'm doing this for your own good."

"But if Jolly——"

"If I had to choose between saving you and Jolly, I would save you," said Grice, and his tone hardened. "But don't make any mistake, we're looking for Jolly."

"If anything happens to him, I'll hold you responsible," Rollison said, harshly. "Don't make any mistake. You'll be responsible. On my own, I could find him."

"I don't believe you could in your present condition," Grice said.

Rollison put the receiver down, holding it very tightly, resisting an impulse to slam it. He stood staring at the Trophy Wall, on which Jolly had worked with such thoroughness; the Trophy Wall had become Jolly's labour of love. Rollison went to the cocktail cabinet, poured out a drink, then put the glass down. Whisky slopped over the side of the glass. Welling had warned him not to drink and he had to take that advice.

He had to get out.

He went to the window, and looked into Gresham Terrace. The two detectives were standing on the other side of the road, talking. Two of Ebbutt's men were on this side of the road—Rollison could just see them. They were youngish fellows, and he recognised one of them as Ted Clark, the son of one of Blacker's oldest enemies. So Clark and Jacoby were on duty.

He began to frown.

They were young. They didn't really know Ebbutt well, and were much less likely to be dominated by Ebbutt than was Percy Wrightson. If they were approached in the

right way, it ought to be possible to persuade them to dis
tract the detectives, and give him a chance to get away.
If he did, though, Grice might carry out his threat, and
charge him. That would be a newspaper sensation, which
wouldn't matter; it would also keep him out of action fo
a week, because he would almost certainly be remanded
in custody. Grice wouldn't go in for half measures.

If he could persuade Ebbutt's two men to fool Grice'
officers, it would be worth it. He couldn't stay here doing
nothing.

Why not have Lola do the distracting? His heart began
to pound at the thought of Lola working on the Yard
men, and Jacoby and Clark coming with him to Ticky
Mendelsohn's. That was the obvious thing to do. Give
him an hour with Ticky, and he would get the information
he needed. Getting out of here, seeing the man, using
strong arm methods if necessary, had become an ob
session. Lola *must* help him.

Rollison strode along the passage, banged on her door
and thrust it open. She was sitting on the dressing-table
stool, wearing only panties, brassière and stockings, and
she looked round towards him; even in that moment
when nothing really mattered but getting out of the apart
ment, his gaze was drawn to her thrusting bosom, and he
was momentarily checked.

She had a lipstick in her hand.

"Richard, darling," she said, "you ought to close the
door."

He slammed it. "I want your help, Lola."

"There isn't anything I wouldn't do for you."

"I told you I wouldn't tell you what I was planning to
do," said Rollison, jerkily. "I've changed my mind.
want to talk to Mendelsohn, alone."

"Of course you do," said Lola. "You didn't have to
tell me that."

He caught his breath—and as he stared, realised that
she was right, that going to Mendelsohn was the obvious

thing to do, and because it was so obvious, it might be the wrong one. His mind began to work more quickly. He had to fool Grice, the Yard men, everyone; if his intentions were as obvious as this, he would get nowhere.

He forced a smile, as Lola stood up, and took that seductive dressing-gown off the end of the bed.

"Hold this for me," she said.

He moved towards her, and she held out the gown. It looked beautiful, even when empty. She smiled at Rollison and turned round slowly, so that her back was towards him. She was standing in front of the three-mirror dressing-table, and the reflections of her body as she turned round, and then as she held her arms backwards, so that he could slip the sleeves over them, made his heart pound. He told himself that she was doing this deliberately; that she could make an absolute fool of him if he allowed her to, and yet—she *was* irresistible. She was absolutely irresistible. She knew it.

She was very close, arms still held backwards—as they would be if she were going to dive off the edge of a swimming pool. The twist of her body as she turned round, the gleam in her eyes, the mirrored reflection that made four of her, all these things were conceived to make him forget everything else—Jolly, Mendelsohn, Grice, Blacker. She meant him to think only of her, and there wasn't a man living who could reject her.

"Richard," she said, "I'm getting cold."

Rollison said: "It's so cold, my clothes are sticking to me." With a swift movement he thrust the gown forward. He didn't put it on her, or fasten the gown at the neck but let it hang from her shoulders, draping the beauty of her figure. He stared at the reflection of her eyes, frowning, fighting against losing his temper. "Lola, I need your help," he repeated.

"Do you, Richard?"

"There are two of Grice's policemen outside. I want you to distract their attention while I go out."

"On your own?"

"There are two of Ebbutt's men downstairs. They will help me."

"Are you sure?"

He wanted to shout: "Of course I'm sure!" Instead, he forced a tight-lipped smile, and said: "I've been handling men like that for a long time."

"I guess you have," she said, musingly. "And you want me to distract Grice's men?"

"Yes."

"I don't know that I should," she said. "I really don't, Rolly."

"For God's sake don't stand there posturing! Go and get rid of them."

She said: "All right, Richard, I'll talk to them." She shrugged the gown off her shoulders, and stretched her arm out for her dress; and now she made no attempt to beguile Rollison. He got the impression that his outburst had angered her, but that she was trying not to show it.

She slipped into the dress, fastened the zip at the side, ran a comb lightly through her hair, then pushed her feet into some evening shoes. She gave him a broad, glassy smile; he had never known her so aloof, or so remote. He opened the door for her, and she went out, leaving a faint trace of perfume behind her. He followed her to the front door, and opened it.

"How do you intend to go about it?" he asked.

"I shall think of a way," she assured him, and went out. He watched her going down the stairs; her head and shoulders did not move, it was almost as if she were floating. She disappeared. Rollison turned round to find Wrightson just behind him.

"Not going out, Mr Ar, are you?"

Rollison didn't answer, but pushed past him into the big room. Wrightson went back to the kitchen the other way, Jolly's way.

Jolly. Rollison felt sweat on his forehead, and on his

upper lip—sweat of anxiety for his man. He must not put a foot wrong. For the first time, he thought of the danger of defying Welling and Grice. He had thought he was being so clever, but in fact Lola had known at once that he would try to get to Mendelsohn, and Hanbury must have known. Grice might find out, too. He, the Toff, doing the obvious at a time like this, when every move had to be so swift and so shrewd that it would outwit the opposition.

Remember, he didn't really know who the opposition was yet. He needed to get to Mendelsohn, or to someone who would know the whole truth—including the truth of Lola's parentage. He could not be sure that he could trust her. There had been the attacks on her, but he had to remind himself that she might have arranged them herself, making sure that she wouldn't be hurt. But—why *should* she? What purpose could she have in making herself appear to be the victim of attacks?

Forget her for the moment. Remember Jolly—almost certainly a prisoner somewhere in London. The possibility that he was dead was too appalling to contemplate. As that thought entered his head, Rollison realised that he was deliberately blinding himself to the obvious possibilities, was refusing to face up to the situation. That blasted drug!

He made himself move towards the window, and looked out, to see Lola talking to the Yard men. She turned, and looked up at him, as if she knew that he would be watching. Then she turned round and came back, walking with that floating motion. The man stayed where they were. Soon, she was at the front door, and he let her in.

"Well?" he asked.

Lola said: "They told me that if they let you leave here your life wouldn't be worth a dime," she said. "I warned them that you would probably try, and——"

He could have struck her.

He swung away, and as he strode back into the big

room, the telephone bell rang. He heard but ignored it.
He knew that Lola was following him, but did not look
round. It went on and on. He moved to the corner cupboard and picked up the whisky—and Wrightson appeared in the doorway, like a ghost of Jolly.

"You told me the Doc said that would only make you
worse," he remarked. "You going to answer the phone or
shall I?"

Rollison could have thrown the glass, whisky and all, at
the man. He held it so tightly that the tension at his
fingers hurt. Lola was standing watching him. The bell
kept ringing, and Wrightson made himself move, and
picked it up. He used the *h* with a kind of nervous gusto.

"The *H*on. Mr Roll'son's residence."

It was like a mimicry of Jolly.

". . . 'Oo wants him?"

There was another pause, and in it Rollison saw Wrightson's attitude change. One moment he had been uneasy
and wary of Rollison, but the next all his attention was
diverted to the speaker at the other end of the line. He
shot a quick, startled glance at Rollison, and said:

"Yes, 'e's 'ere. 'Ang on."

Wrightson put the receiver down slowly. Rollison
hadn't moved, and couldn't think who would have had
such an effect on him. Then the expression in Wrightson's
eyes seemed to declare the truth. This was news about
Jolly! This was Grice, with news——

He strode across and snatched the receiver.

"Rollison here."

"Good evening, sir," said Jolly.

20

PRESSURE

"WHERE the devil have you got to?" Rollison demanded harshly. "We've been hunting for you all over London."

Jolly said, very quietly: "That I can well believe, sir."

"Where are you?"

"I'm afraid I don't know."

"Now look here, I've had enough of this. I don't want to play hunt the thimble. Where are——?"

Rollison broke off, abruptly. Wrightson moved away from the room, and Rollison was just aware of the fact that Lola followed him. It was one development after another, and he couldn't *do* anything; he needed physical action, he needed fresh air, he needed to clear his head of confusion.

"What do you mean, you don't know, Jolly?" His voice was much quieter.

"I'm afraid that is the truth, sir. I am being kept here against my will. I think it is an old house in London, but I can't be absolutely positive of that. It is a working class home, and I know that between half past five and six o'clock a lot of people passed by, as they would after a day's work."

Rollison said: "Are you all right?"

"A little drowsy, sir—I was drugged. Very foolishly I allowed myself to be beguiled into carrying an elderly person's shopping bag into Hator Mews, near Shepherd Market, and a closed van was waiting. I had no chance to save myself." There was a brief pause, and in it Rollison tried to decide what sensible thing to say. Before he made up his mind, Jolly went on: "I don't think you need worry about me, sir——"

There was a sharp exclamation, a kind of scuffling sound, and then another voice came on the line, a muffled one, obviously that of a man speaking through a piece of gauze, to disguise the sound.

"Don't you take any notice of Jolly," he said. "You've got plenty to worry about unless you do what you're told. If you want to see Jolly again, do it and do it quick. That clear?"

Rollison said: "Yes."

"It had better be. Get it straight, Rollison—it's Jolly's life if you don't do what you're told."

"I understand."

The man said: "Will you do it?"

"Just tell me what you want."

There was a pause. It dragged on and on, and Rollison felt his own tension increasing, felt the sweat standing out on his forehead, felt his teeth clenching. Lola appeared just in front of him, and her fingers rested very gently on the back of his left hand, which was clenching and bunched on the table.

There was a gasp; as of a man being hurt.

Then, Jolly spoke again.

"Are you—are you there, sir?"

"Yes."

"I thought there was a chance to get to the front door, but I misjudged the distance," Jolly said. "May I beg you not to do what this man asks? I beg you not to."

"I don't know what he wants yet," Rollison said. "Are you all right?"

"I caught a blow on the face, sir, but not at all serious," said Jolly. "The—the instruction is quite impossible."

"Let me be the judge."

"Okay, Rollison," the other man said, and Rollison realised that he had an ear-piece extension. "It's simple, and it won't take long. Kill Lola Davenport."

Rollison drew in his breath.

Jolly said clearly, although some distance from the mouthpiece: "You must not think of it for a moment, sir. I have told this man that you won't even consider it."

"Get it?" demanded the man with the muffled voice.
"Kill Lola Davenport. I don't care how you do it. Cut
her throat or strangle her or put poison in her Manhattan
Cocktail. You can push her under a bus or throw her out
of the window for all I care, but if she isn't dead by this
time tomorrow, Jolly will be. It's half past nine. Don't
make any mistake, I mean what I say."

"Mr Rollison!" Jolly called, as if he were even further
away from the mouthpiece. "It is unthinkable, it——"

The receiver went down with a clang.

Rollison kept his receiver pressed close to his ear for
a moment, and then looked into Lola's eyes. Obviously
she didn't know what had been said; she couldn't know.
Her eyes were clear blue, and their expression was gentle;
she looked at him as might a woman in love. She didn't
smile, but was very grave.

"Come and sit down," she said.

Rollison didn't move; his whole body felt stiff.

"What did he say?" asked Lola, still gently.

Rollison said: "Forget it." He moistened his lips, freed
himself, went to the corner cupboard, picked up the
whisky and soda, and tossed it down. He stood staring at
Lola. The man's voice seemed to be hovering about inside
his head. 'Cut her throat or strangle her or put poison in
her Manhattan Cocktail. You can push her under a bus
or throw her out of the window for all I care, but if she
isn't dead by this time tomorrow, Jolly will be.'

Lola said: "It can't be as bad as you seem to
think."

"Can't it?" said Rollison, harshly.

"Richard, you're not well——"

"I don't have to be bursting with rude health to know
how bad this situation is."

"Is Jolly all right?"

"So far."

"Then what——"

Rollison's head was beginning to throb, and as he

stared at Lola he remembered what Welling had told him; that if he drank spirits he was likely to get a severe headache, and that it would linger on for hours. How big a fool could he be? Where was Jolly, and who was the man who wanted Lola dead?

"I know you think I'm bothering you, but I wish you would sit down," said Lola. "Why don't you tell me what he said?"

"It wasn't good," said Rollison. He tried to make his voice less harsh, and even smiled. "Remember—nobody but nobody has to know what he said to me." He felt that he must sit down, and moved towards his chair. He thought that Lola was going to help him, and felt a flash of irritation, but she simply moved a book so that he would not knock it off the arm. He dropped down, his head thumping, his legs feeling weak. He closed his eyes and said:

"Did Grice tell you that they've doped me?"

"Have they?"

"Yes. Very clever, wasn't it?"

"These people *are* very clever."

"Yes. Cleverer than you might think. There was just one person in the world who could help me out of this fix and who would see it my way. That's Jolly. So they snatched Jolly."

"What do they want you to do?"

"Help them to make a lot of money," said Rollison. "I have to go over on their side, and join the ranks of crime, or they will kill Jolly. Don't ask me whether they mean it; of course they mean it."

"I should imagine they mean everything they say," agreed Lola. "Is it to do with me?"

"Why should it be?"

Lola said: "Do they want you to murder me, Richard?"

Could she have heard? Could that muffled voice have carried so far from the ear-piece? Or was she simply making a shrewd guess? She was nobody's fool. Nobody but nobody. What had made him think of that piece of nonsense? She must think that he was out of his wits.

He opened his eyes to look at her, and she was sitting on the edge of a low chair, knees and ankles close together, beautiful beyond words; beautiful beyond imagination. She was looking at him gravely, and he remembered suspecting that in some tortuous way she might be the instigator of all this. It couldn't be true, now. She wouldn't give anybody instructions to tell him to kill her. Nonsense, nonsense, nonsense. But there must be logic in the whole affair, a clue to it, which he had not yet seen but which would explain everything simply. Simply. That was what he needed, a simple explanation.

His eyes were heavy.

My God!

He grabbed the arms of the chair and sprang to his feet—and staggered and swayed as he did so. Lola sat looking up at him.

"Lola!" he cried out.

"It's all right, Richard," Lola said quietly. "Dr Welling said that you must have some rest—I talked to him on the telephone. He said that if you didn't you might become seriously ill, or else——"

"What do you mean, Welling said I must rest? What have you done? What——"

"Richard, there's nothing to worry about," said Lola, very firmly. "I put some tablets into your drink—the one you had just now. They were medically prescribed, and Dr Welling——"

"You—you crafty bitch! You——" Rollison took a step towards her, but did not trust his legs.

"I don't mind what you call me, Richard," Lola said, and instead of trying to get further away from him, got up and came towards him. "I want to help you, and I'm not very interested in anything else." She took his arm and guided him back to the chair, and he knew that he hadn't the strength to fight against her. He could not be sure that she was telling the truth, and yet—someone wanted him to kill her. If he didn't, Jolly would die. Wouldn't she want him alive, to help her, to help Jolly? Why should she put him out of action now unless she was carrying out the doctor's orders?

Damn Welling, he would never be called to this flat again.

He was sitting down.

Lola perched herself on the arm of his chair.

"Rolly," she said, "Dr Welling said that if you had a long rest, by tomorrow you might be much more your-self—there was a drug in that whisky intended to counter-act the first. If you just relax, you'll have a better chance of being yourself again tomorrow."

She was smoothing his hand with hers.

"Don't fight against it," she urged. "Don't fight against it. The police will find Jolly, and I will . . ."

He was going under. She was trying to make it easy, but with or without her, he was losing consciousness, and his mind was now so dulled that he felt neither anger nor resentment; even his anxiety for Jolly was less urgent. Her hand was very soft.

"Lola——"

"Don't worry about anything, Richard."

"Tell the—tell the police to—to question Ticky . . . Ticky . . ."

"Mendelsohn. I'll tell them."

"Very important," Rollison muttered. "Very impor-tant." He felt his eyes so heavy that he knew he was almost gone, and he could not get any impression of anxiety into his voice. He wanted to speak Lola's name again, but the muscles at his lips relaxed, and he could not. His body was going limp everywhere. "Lo——" he began, and then his head slumped to his chest.

*   *   *

"Will he be all right, Miss?" Wrightson asked anxi-ously.

"I hope so, I really hope so," Lola answered. "Will you help me to carry him into his room?"

"Don't need no 'elp for that," said Wrightson. He moved forward and hoisted Rollison out of the chair and over his shoulder with what seemed like sleight of hand. Then he turned and strode towards the bedrooms. "Bin an Auxiliary Fireman for twenty years," he explained. "Carried coves twice as 'eavy as Mr Ar down the fire escape a dozen times, and gorn back for more. You turn the bed down, then I'll get 'is clothes off. Might as well make him comfy while we're about it."

"I'll look after him now, Percy," said Lola.

Wrightson looked at her as if he was not sure that it was quite proper; then grinned, shrugged, dumped Rollison on the bed and stood back. "Well I don't mind admitting that if he 'ad 'is choice, 'e'd go for you as a nurse rarver than me. Want any 'elp?"

"I shall want something to eat afterwards."

"Don't you worry," said Wrightson. "I'm ravenous meself." He went towards the door, and said over his shoulder: "I 'ope to Gawd 'e's all right, Miss. And I 'ope Jolly——"

He broke off and disappeared.

For a moment Lola bent over Rollison, without touching him. Then she began to loosen his collar. She was taking off his tie when Wrightson coughed loudly from the door.

"Don't get me wrong, Miss," he said briskly. "I 'ope you come aht of it all right, too."

21

ROLLISON WAKES

ROLLISON opened his eyes to darkness which was not wholly dark, and did not understand why. He lay in bed for a few minutes, trying to think, trying to remember what had happened, and it came back slowly. His reaction surprised him, for some reason which he did not understand, either; he accepted the situation calmly. He ought to be angry; he was not. Yet his mind was working smoothly, and recollection was coming back . . . How Lola had talked in the few minutes before he had lost consciousness, for instance. How angry he had been with her, how near he had come to striking her.

Jolly?

He felt the stirring of anxiety; not anger, anxiety.

He looked round at the window, which was alongside the head of the bed, and saw that the curtains were drawn, but that at one spot there was a glow of light. He realised that it was daylight outside, but someone had done a very good job of darkening the room; a much better job than usual.

He hitched himself up on his pillows, ran his fingers through his hair, and then listened intently. He could hear no sound. He pictured Lola, and wondered where she was—and what was the truth about her. At last, he got out of bed.

His legs were quite steady, but his movements were a little sluggish. He went to the window and found that the curtains had been fastened with safety pins. He smiled as he undid several of these. The curtains fell to one side, and the bright evening sunlight came in; judging from those shadows, it was about the same time as it had been when he had woken the previous evening. Half past six. And Jolly——

Alarm stabbed through him; the man on the telephone had allowed him twenty-four hours, or until nine o'clock. On the instant he felt a great sense of urgency. He swung round towards the door, strode across to it, turned the handle and pulled—but the door did not open. He pulled again, stared down, and remembered how thorough Lola could be. The key was turned in the other side of the lock. Last night, he would have been in a flaming temper about this; now he was able to smile, if ruefully.

"You're certainly keeping me quiet," he said *sotto voce*.

He went to his bedside table. His clothes must have been folded and put away, but the contents of his pockets had been put neatly on that table; neatness seemed to be part of Lola's character. Among the oddments was his knife, with the picklock blade. He grinned; there were things she didn't know about.

But instead of opening the door at once, he turned on the cold tap at the handbasin, rinsed his face thoroughly, but making little noise, and plugged in the electric razor. Suddenly, he decided that it would make too much noise, so he shaved with a safety razor.

Someone walked briskly past the door; that would be Percy Wrightson or one of Ebbutt's men. There was no sound of voices.

Rollison washed again, still very quietly, and dressed. He put all the things from the table into his pocket, then went to his wardrobe, unlocked the drawer at the bottom, took out several of the tear-gas phials, and after a moment's hesitation, an automatic pistol. He checked that this was loaded, and slipped an extra clip of ammunition into his pocket. Finally, he picked up a kind of bracelet, which had a narrow sheath attached. He clipped the bracelet round his right arm a few inches below the elbow, and put a knife into the sheath, so that it did not interfere with his movements. This was the kind of armoury he would have taken with him on Commando raids during the war; there seemed nothing strange about it.

He opened the skeleton key blade of his knife, and unlocked the door without difficulty. He stepped into the passage, and glanced into the guest room; it was empty, but Lola's things were on the dressing-table. He went into the big room, and saw Lola sitting in an armchair, her legs up on a pouffe; she was reading. Then he saw that she was studying some of the press cutting books which Jolly kept up to date—there were twenty and more of them, one for each year of the Toff's activities as what Lola would call a private eye. The press cuttings were companion pieces to the trophies on the wall.

Rollison moved silently over the carpet, and was just behind her when he said:

"I always thought that account was exaggerated. What do you think?"

Lola started violently, and swung round. The book slipped off her knees to the floor. She started to get up, but Rollison moved forward and pressed her shoulders down.

"Hallo," he said. "What day is it?"

"Richard! I didn't hear you."

"You weren't supposed to hear me. How long have I been under? Since last night?"

"Yes."

"Only last night?"

"Yes."

"So Jolly has three hours left." Now Rollison's heart began to thump, for obviously there was a possibility that there was more news of Jolly.

"It's terrible, Rolly. Just terrible."

"The police haven't found him, then?" Rollison said heavily.

"No," replied Lola. "Rolly, let me stand up." He took his hands away, and she jumped to her feet. She scanned his features closely, especially his eyes, as if looking for some sign in them. "How are you feeling? Are you all right?"

"I'm fine. I don't hate you any more, either. I could learn to, if you are difficult, but—let's have it, Lola. Is there any development? Have the police made any discovery? Is the Moodys' killer caught?"

Lola said: "No. No, nothing good——"

"Is Jolly dead?" Rollison demanded, suddenly harsh, and he was terribly afraid.

"No," Lola answered chokily. "No, there's no news of Jolly. But the man Mendelsohn?"

"Yes?" Rollison almost shouted.

"He's disappeared. He flew to New York, and hasn't been traced from there." Lola broke off, and looked almost fearful, as if she guessed how much that would upset Rollison.

"Nothing else?"

"No, nothing," Lola assured him. "Bill Grice called me half-an-hour ago, and told me about Mendelsohn. He said——" She broke off.

"Go on," urged Rollison.

"Rolly," Lola said, almost as if it were against her will, "Grice said he was terribly worried and he said that there had never been a time when you were more necessary."

"Good old Bill," said Rollison. "Do you think we could persuade him to let me out now?"

"I should think so," Lola said. "I can't be sure, but——"

"That's what worries me," said Rollison. "He may believe that I could take him straight to Jolly, like a pigeon on its homing instinct, but he would probably need a medical certificate from Doc Welling to say that I was fit and of sound mind."

"I don't understand you," Lola said. "You're so different. You're so much calmer."

"That's right," said Rollison. "Doc Welling's pills did the trick. I not only have a mind now, but I can use it. I want to get out of here. I know exactly where to go and what to do, but I don't think it would be helped if

Grice's or Ebbutt's men followed me, though I could find a use for Clark and Jacoby. Are they on duty now?"

"Yes," she said. "And—and Bill Ebbutt came this afternoon. I've never seen a man look more anxious. He seemed to think that Jolly is dead."

"Bill always did look on the gloomy side. Have there been any more threats?"

"Yes," answered Lola. "Yes." She closed her eyes, and Rollison thought that she looked on the point of exhaustion. Frightened? "Richard, you'll find out sooner or later, you had better know now." The words increased his tension but he showed no outward sign. "This man has been telephoning Ebbutt, as well as several newspapers and—and George Hanbury's office. He's said the same thing every time. That if you don't do what he told you to, he'll kill Jolly by half past nine tonight."

Rollison glanced at the clock on the mantelpiece; it was five to seven.

"Two and a half hours," he said, stonily. "There's still time."

"Richard——"

"I've got to get out of here, and I need Clark and Jacoby with me," said Rollison. "And I want the Yard men fooled. You're good at fooling men."

Lola said: "Richard, I've been trying not to fool myself. I've been trying to find a way out of this awful situation. I feel responsible for having involved you, and——"

"Oh, no. Blame Blacker."

"It doesn't matter who we blame, I still feel responsible," Lola said, in a sharper voice. "And—it's Jolly's life or mine. Isn't that what it comes to?"

"It seems to."

"Richard," said Lola, now speaking very quickly, "don't make any mistake. I want to live. But God knows I can understand how you feel about Jolly. There must be some way out of this predicament—and—and I think I've found one way. I lay awake most of last night thinking

about it, and I've been concentrating on it all day. This—
this man told you to kill me, or he would kill Jolly, didn't
he?"

"Yes," confirmed Rollison very softly. He understood
what made her look so tired, now, but could only guess
what was in her mind, and he had to be sure before he
made any comment.

"It can only be for one reason," Lola went on. "He
wants me to die so that the Blacker money goes on to
someone else. Isn't that right?"

"It could be."

"Supposing I refuse to take the inheritance?" asked
Lola. "Supposing I say that since I've been in England
I've discovered that this is blood money, and won't have
any of it? Supposing I just back down, Rolly? Would
that—would that solve the problem?"

Rollison stood staring at her for a long time; for a
precious minute, at the very least. Then he began to
smile. He stepped close to her, slid his arms round
her, and crushed her to him; and he said into her
ear:

"That really makes you the perfect woman. But no,
sweetheart, no, it wouldn't solve the problem. This chap
wants you dead. Don't fool yourself."

She said: "I—I can't—think of another thing." She
looked at him as he stood away from her, and suddenly glanced at the Trophy Wall. In a tone almost of
desperation. she said: "You say you're fond of Jolly.
He's been your servant all your life, and he means everything to you. I don't mean a thing, Richard. I can't mean
a thing. Why don't you—why don't you kill me? It
would be easy. You would be able to blame it on to
someone else. You're clever enough to do that. If you
have to chose between Jolly and me, why——?" she
broke off.

Rollison said, softly: "The wicked Queen of Strip. The
hard-bitten Broadway Seductress Who Rose From the

Slums of Brooklyn. Lola, I've never been so near telling a woman that I loved her and was in love with her. But you've made a slight mistake in your reasoning."

She didn't respond.

Rollison went on: "It isn't a question of choosing between you and Jolly. It's a simple issue, an issue which a lot of people would call naïve, but no other really counts. It's a question of choosing between what's right and what's wrong. If we gave Jolly a choice of being shot, or knowing that you were to be killed so that he could be freed, he wouldn't hesitate; he's taken the thought of death philosophically. Now! Listen to me, sweet. I want those Yard men fooled, and I think that can be simple, too. I want you to go down to the street and tell them I've disappeared. They'll come hurrying in, and——" He was beginning to smile.

"But where are you going?"

"I'll tell you when we're on the way," said Rollison. "Let's get a plan worked out so that it's almost foolproof. We need a car, and mine won't do, but Jolly has a Morris Minor nearby. Is Percy Wrightson here?"

"Yes."

"Percy will be more amenable now," declared Rollison. "Give him this bunch of keys. One's for the garage, Number 3, Hator Mews. The other is for the ignition. Tell him to have it facing Piccadilly, at the end of Hator Mews, double-parked. Then go downstairs and talk to Clark and Jacoby. Tell them to get a taxi as soon as the Yard men have come in here, and to follow me in the Morris Minor. They can pick me up at the Brook Street end of Piccadilly."

"You said I was coming with you!"

"When Grice's men are up here, you simply go down to the street again and hurry to the Morris," Rollison said. "I'll be in it. Once everything is laid on, all we'll need is a few minutes' grace. We aren't going very far."

"Where *are* we going?"

"I think, to Jolly," Rollison said.

*   *   *

Twenty minutes later, from the window of the big room, Rollison saw Lola talking to Grice's men, apparently in a great state of agitation. He was half-way down the stairs leading from the apartment when he heard the men hurrying in from the street, and heard Lola saying: "We've looked everywhere in the flat, we simply can't find him."

Rollison stepped into the doorway of the flat immediately beneath his, and stood facing it. He was wearing one of Jolly's bowler hats and Wrightson's old raincoat. The Yard men and Lola hurried past him, and from the open door of his own flat, he heard Wrightson call anxiously:

"You found 'im?"

"No, we have not," called Lola, as if desperately.

Rollison stepped softly back to the staircase and walked without haste down the stairs. As he stepped into the street, he saw a taxi stop at the far end, and the two young men who had reason to hate Blacker for what the man had done to their fathers get into it. Everything was going like clockwork.

Keeping to this side of the road so that there was less chance of being seen by the Yard men if they looked out of the window, he lengthened his stride, reached the corner, and saw Jolly's grey Morris Minor waiting for him; it was too late for the Traffic Wardens to be on duty. He got into the driving seat and started the engine, then nosed the car along towards Gresham Terrace. He reached the corner as Lola appeared. She didn't say a word as she scrambled into the car and pulled the door to.

Rollison turned on to Piccadilly, turned left, passed the end of the next street, and saw Ebbutt's two men, in the taxi, turn after him. It was a little after half past seven, and nothing had gone wrong.

There were two hours to work in.

Lola said: "I want to know where we're going, Richard, please."

"So you shall," said Rollison. "The one obvious place, the only place conceivable. I started getting short-tempered after drinking coffee at George Hanbury's office. He had the opportunity to slip the drug into sugar and milk at the apartment. He had the opportunity to take that hammer. He could have killed the Moodys—remember, it was obviously done by someone who was familiar with the place; Hanbury had been there frequently, and knew the grounds well. Oh, it all adds up to our George. The shocking thing as far as I'm concerned is that when he told me so, I wouldn't listen to him."

Rollison was driving fast through a sprinkling of traffic.

"When he *told* you?"

"Oh, yes," said Rollison. "He told me first through you and then to my face. He said that he and old Mrs Regson had heard Blacker and Ticky Mendelsohn planning revenge. In short, he told me to go and see Mendelsohn. What he was really saying was: 'Suspect everyone except me.' Later he said that he would betray a client's confidence—any solicitor prepared to do that must be three parts rogue. And I was under the influence of the drug, so couldn't see the obvious."

Lola said: "Can you be sure?"

"I'll be sure, if Jolly's in the flat above Gammon and Hanbury's office," said Rollison heavily.

22

GRAN

No one was about in Lincoln's Inn.

The Morris Minor pulled up behind two other parked cars, and the taxi a little way behind it. Rollison waited until Ebbutt's two men had paid off the cabby, and then got out of the car. Lola was on the other side. It was the first time Rollison had been face to face with Clark and Jacoby, and he liked what he saw. They were obviously as hard as nails, the type of young boxer Ebbutt trained well, clear-eyed, ready to tackle anything. They had learned the value of obedience from Ebbutt, and Rollison had no doubt that they would do what they were told.

"You two had better split up," Rollison said. "One of you stay at the front here. The other go along that passage"—he pointed—"and he'll find a back entrance to all the houses and offices here. The numbers are on the back doors; you want to be near Number 62."

Jacoby, tall, dark-haired, blue eyed, said: "Okay with me. I take the back, Ted?"

"Suits me," said Clark. He was half smiling, half frowning. "What do you expect to happen, Mr Rollison?"

"Young Hanbury might come running in either direction," said Rollison. "He might have others with him. I——"

He broke off; and felt first shocked, and then triumphant.

Parked a few yards along was a pale-blue motor-scooter, of the make he had seen outside the New Forest inn. He studied the stickers on the windshield, and saw that one was an AAA sign, stuck in exactly the same place as the one he had noticed in Hampshire.

"Is that the machine?" Lola demanded.

"Yes, for sure," answered Rollison. "Lola, will you go and telephone Scotland Yard, and tell Grice that I'm here?"

She hesitated.

"There comes a time when Grice has to know," Rollison said. "This is it."

"I—I want to come upstairs with you."

"Oh, no," said Rollison. "Not if I have to chain you to the railings. If I'm right about this, the killer will make a final attempt at you, and he might succeed. It won't help me or anyone else to know that he'll never get his hands on your half million. If anyone gets his hands on you and yours," added Rollison with a glint in his eyes, "it will be me."

Lola said: "I want to come with you."

"Lola," said Rollison, "there's a chance that I can get Jolly out alive. If you're with me, I'll have you on my hands, and I might lose both of you. Find a telephone kiosk and call the Yard."

She said, almost humbly: "All right, Rolly," and turned away.

Rollison went to the front door of Number 62. Two men with furled umbrellas and bowler hats, who looked as if they were prepared for a downpour, walked briskly past, without glancing their way. Lola looked round, twice. Jacoby had gone to the back, and Clark was near the Morris Minor. Rollison took out his skeleton key, stood with his back to the others and worked on the lock. It soon turned. He opened the door and stepped inside, then closed the door as quickly as he had opened it. Some light came in through the fanlight. He stood listening before moving forward cautiously. He heard no sound.

He walked up the stairs, keeping close to the wall so as to prevent the boards from creaking. At the first landing, he stopped to look down; nothing moved, and all he could see was the dim light and paintwork which needed attention. At the next landing, a sign on the wall, pointing upwards, said:

"*Caretaker—No Offices.*"

He checked the doors of the offices at this landing and made sure that all were locked, and then started up the stairs. There was nothing to suggest that anyone had heard. He rounded the turn in the stairs, and looked upwards. Two doors were above him, one at the end and one at the side of a small landing. Still keeping very quiet he reached this landing. One door was marked: *Caretaker*, and the other: *Private*. Now, he heard the sound of a voice. He listened intently, and came to the conclusion that it was someone on the radio. That helped; he could risk making a little noise.

Of course, he might be wrong; Jolly might not be here. It was after eight o'clock, and there was desperately little time. If he had made a mistake, if in fact he should have tried Mendelsohn's place—no, the police would have done that by now, it was too obvious.

Rollison took out the skeleton key, and began to work on the lock. He felt it give; it was quite a simple kind, with a large keyhole, not one which would ever keep an expert cracksman out. He eased it as slowly as he could but it fell back with a sharp *click*. He drew the skeleton key out and stepped away from the door, but the radio voice went on and on, and nothing suggested that anyone had heard him. He turned the handle of the door and pushed.

The door opened, the voice came more clearly; it was a BBC speaker, there was no longer any doubt. Rollison stepped inside, on to a rough hair or coconut matting carpet. Two doors led off the room beyond, one of them closed and one of them ajar; it was through this door that he heard the radio. He stepped towards it, and looked through. The old woman was sitting in an armchair, staring in front of her, thin hands on the arms. The radio was on a shelf near her head. The room was a living-room, with a gas stove and a sink in one corner; a folded screen was by this.

No one else was here.

So the only hope now was that Jolly was in the room with the closed door. Rollison crept away from the living-room, went to the door and tried the handle. It was locked. He took out the knife again, opened the blade, and started to work. This lock was more intricate, but it would not take more than two or three minutes to force. He kept stopping, to listen, but the radio speaker drowned any other sound, and he felt more confident with every passing second. He felt the skeleton key catch, and knew that he would have the door open in a moment.

He prayed that Jolly was in there.

He turned the lock.

Mrs Regson spoke from the partly open door.

"Just turn round, Mister Rollison. Turn round and look at me."

He gripped the handle of the door more tightly for it might distract her if he flung it open. He did not know whether she was carrying a weapon, and in any case, she was a frail creature. He felt sure that the man involved was probably near, and he wanted to make the man and also the woman speak. They were more likely to if they thought him helpless. He put one of the fragile tear-gas phials into his mouth and tucked it cautiously to one side with his tongue. As he finished, he heard a click and a roar. He started violently, but the phial was safe. A thud of sound came from the door close by him, and he saw wood splintering in front of his eyes. The end of a bullet showed in the flimsy door.

"Would you like the next one in your back?" the old woman demanded.

Very slowly, Rollison turned round. There she was, just as he had seen her before, her hair done in a bun at the back, her face showing traces of a youthful beauty. But her eyes were no longer vague and lack-lustre. She held the gun firmly, and there was no doubt she would shoot him if he gave her any cause.

"Come towards me," she ordered. "Take three steps."

He obeyed her.

He stood silently for a moment, watching her features; as he did so, the door opened behind him, and a man said, in a high-pitched voice:

"That caught him, Gran. Now we've got him. This is the end of Mr Bloody Toff."

*   *   *

Rollison watched the gun in the old woman's hand, but listened for the movements of the man behind him. He could sense that the other was very near, heard a rustle of sound, and felt the man's hands at his pocket. The gun was pulled out, and the man laughed. Then Rollison felt a hand at his arm, and realized that this man knew about the knife. Gus Blacker had been one of the few men to find out about that; had he passed his knowledge on?

The man said: "Take your coat off."

Rollison obeyed, slowly.

The old woman said: "So your grandfather knew what he was talking about," and the man unclasped the bracelet and the knife.

The other tear-gas phials were in the coat, so now Rollison's only weapon was the one in his mouth.

He felt a sharp kick behind his right leg, taking him completely by surprise. His knee bent and he staggered and nearly fell. As he was staggering, the man behind him pushed him to one side, and as he fetched up against a chair, stood sneering at him.

It was the motor-cyclist from the New Forest inn, a man with small features, a rather pointed chin, and narrowed eyes. Now he was grinning, but there was tension in his expression, a curious fox-like curl to his lips. He stood with his hands at his hips.

"So you let an old woman fool you," he jeered,

and raised his voice. "That's a laugh, that is—ain't it, Gran?"

"It would make your grandfather laugh himself sick," the woman said.

"You're telling me," sneered the youth. He was probably in the early twenties, and there was nothing good-looking about him. He moved further away from Rollison and looked him up and down. "So the great Toff's done for. How about that? The Toff and his bootlicker, *Mister* Jolly. I'll look after the gentleman, Gran. You go and get Jolly."

He stretched out his hand for the gun, and the old woman gave it to him. She passed Rollison, thrust out her hand and scratched his cheek. Thank God it was the other side from the phial. She gave a high-pitched laugh as Rollison backed away, wincing with the sudden pain. "*Jolly, Jolly, Mister Jolly!*" she called, cackling, and disappeared into the room behind Rollison. He made no attempt to move, knowing that when he did move it must be decisively; there was not the slightest hope of a second chance.

"Jolly, Jolly, Mister Jolly!" the woman called, as if she were calling a cat.

She came in, holding Jolly by the right arm. Jolly was very pale. His eyes looked huge and red-rimmed, as they would from lack of sleep. He kept staggering. Rollison glanced down and saw the way his trousers were wrinkled round the turn-ups, and he realised that he had been bound hand and foot, that lack of circulation was making him unsteady. His hands were still tied behind him. He lost his footing, but the old woman held him upright, then pushed him so that he collapsed into a chair.

He stared mutely at Rollison.

"Hallo, Jolly," Rollison said.

"*Hellow, Joely,*" mimicked the youth.

"Gus," said the old woman, "what about that American bitch?"

"Now we've got Rollison we can look after her," said the youth. "Want to know something, Toff? I was going to phone you if you hadn't come on your own—I bet Gran that you'd cotton on sooner or later, and come after dear old George. Made you think you were after George, Toff, didn't I?"

He came swaggering in front of Rollison. "Well, what's it feel like? It's your turn at last. This is what you did to my old Grandad, remember? You put him in a corner, and then you held him there until the cops arrived. Only the cops won't arrive in time to help you. If they were outside now, I'd have time to finish you off and get clear—but they're nowhere in sight. I can see every gateway from here, and I'd know. But I knew you'd come—Jolly was too juicy a bait for you, that was a dead cert. Like to know how I'm going to finish you all off?"

Rollison said: "Tell me."

"Okay, I'll tell you. There's going to be a leak of gas. You and Jolly and the Babe from Brooklyn will all have a nice long sleep." He glanced across at the gas fire, which had two of its white mantles broken, and then turned back to Rollison. "And if you're telling yourself that the police will get me, you can forget it. Yes, sir, you can forget it. My dear old Grandma will look after that. I'm going to get out. I've got plenty of places to go to. And Gran's going to perjure herself—isn't that terrible? Gran's going to say that the wicked man wot did it was George Hanbury. Because George pinched that hammer—he had to, see? George made a little mistake with some client's money a year ago, and he wouldn't have liked the news to leak out. So he's had to do a number of little things for Gran and me—like helping to fool you, Toff, and helping to fool the Brooklyn Babe, and generally making himself useful. And he'll be here soon. He's going to kill himself. Gran's going to tell your old pal Gricey that Hanbury got all the revenge he wanted when he killed you and Jolly and Lola, but he knew he couldn't get away with it so did away with hisself. Gran's going to be ever so shocked—aren't you, Gran?"

"Everso," mimicked the woman, in a high-pitched voice.

"And just in case you feel like shouting a warning, Toff, I'm going to slap this plaster over your mouth," went on young Gus. He picked up a square of adhesive plaster from a table, and spread it over one hand. "It's quick and neat, too. My Grandpa taught me it. He taught me a lot of things, Gus Blacker did—and he taught me to hate your guts. He always said I was a chip off the old block, like my Dad, but that his other son wasn't worth a sniff. Didn't he, Gran?"

"He didn't think George was worth a sniff," agreed 'Gran'.

"That made you jump, Rollison, didn't it?" jeered the re-incarnation of Gus Blacker. "Yes, George is my uncle. When Grice is told the villain was George he won't be surprised, because Gran will tell him who George is, but she'll forget all about me. Won't you, Gran?"

"Yes, Gus," the old woman said. "Gus, I think you ought to hurry, I think I hear someone."

"Not to worry," said Gus. "When anyone steps on that mat at the front or the one at the back we'll hear the bell. We'll be all ready for Lola." He drew nearer, gun in hand, and held out the plaster towards Rollison. "Take it," he ordered. "Take it and slap it over your own mouth, or——"

Rollison stretched out his left hand. Jolly was staring at him, as if he could not believe he would give in without a fight. Gus made a swift movement, evading Rollison's hand; the plaster was there on his palm, ready to slap it on.

Rollison spat the tear-gas phial into his face.

23

GUS THE SECOND

As Gus the Second reeled away, face smothered in the billowing gas, Rollison snatched at the gun in the youth's left hand, took it away, twisted it round and pointed it at the woman. She was already rushing towards him. He saw the glitter in her eyes, the hatred where there had once seemed vagueness, and while her grandson was coughing and spluttering and staggering, she seemed to gather speed. Rollison realized that she was going to throw herself at him, bullet or no bullet; all she wanted to do was to harm him. He dodged. She tried to slap the gun aside, missed, and kicked out at him. For a moment he thought he would have to grab her ankle and toss her away, as Hanbury had treated Lola.

But she lost her balance as she kicked.

It was pathetic to see her trying to recover, gasping for breath, arms whirling, as pathetic to see the way she collapsed against the wall and slithered down it. On the way she began to sob. She was trying to mouth curses, trying to get up so that she could attack him again, but she hadn't a chance.

Then a bell sounded clearly and next moment footsteps thumped on the stairs. Grice's men were here.

* * *

It did not take long for the police to move old Mrs Regson and Gus the Second out of the flat, or to search it and find all the evidence they needed. There was an old marriage certificate showing that Augustus Blacker and Mary O'Hara had been married in a registry office in County Cork, at the beginning of the First World War. There were certificates showing that there had been two children of this marriage, a son, who had been killed in the Second World War, and another, born several years later, and christened George. There were also certificates showing the birth of a son—one son—to this first son's wife. She had died soon after Blacker's first-born, the son had been left in the care of the grandmother. Soon afterwards George Blacker had taken on the name Hanbury, presumably because he had been brought up by the older Hanbury, as a Ward. There was no explanation of why George was sent away from home.

"It's a long story," Grice told Rollison and Lola, the day after the climax in Lincoln's Inn. "The old woman has told us nearly everything we need to know. She was as bad as Blacker, in her way—she helped Blacker to breed hatred in his grandson."

Lola asked: "Can you breed evil into any man?"

"Nice point," said Rollison, leaning back in his favourite chair. "Some say yes, but I'm inclined to think that when they come as bad as Gus the First and Gus the Second, it's a quality born in them. There was no real evil in George Hanbury. In fact his father had him sent to London with the Hanburys—and George turned against him. That seems to have been a big disappointment to Gus, but he didn't do anything about it. George seems to have lived in a kind of fear that the truth would come out one day. He vacillated from one side to the other, as we know. It isn't really surprising. He was Blacker's son by another woman, Mrs Regson was his step-mother—and had no love for him at all."

"There's one thing I just don't understand," Lola said, leaning forward on a pouffe and hugging her knees. She was wearing a low-cut dress, but did not seem to give a thought to what she was doing to Superintendent Grice, whose gaze kept dropping, and then being sternly averted. "If Blacker left his wife, why did she help him later on?"

Grice said: "I can only tell you what she told me. That Blacker always insisted that the wedding should be kept quiet. He married her because the first child, Gus's father, was on the way, but she was not exactly faithful when he was away, and he told her he would never give her a penny if she ever talked about it or told anyone. She lived in Ireland. He visited her from time to time, and the villagers thought that he was a sailor. He made her a generous allowance, and she was content to leave things as they were. The second child, George, was sent to England early—to go to school, it was said. That wasn't unusual, and aroused little comment.

"It wasn't until near the end of his life that she came to England, and nursed Blacker until he died," went on Grice. "Just how he made her hate you, Rolly, I shall never know, but he managed to make her and his grandson believe that they could not rest easy until you were dead. He had talked over ways and means with young Gus, who had the old man's warped outlook and the same liking for crude practical jokes."

"How about Blacker's money?" Rollison asked. "If he had a lawful grandson in Gus the Second, and Gus was so much like him, why leave the money to Lola?"

Now Lola turned her face towards Grice, who had no trouble in looking into her eyes.

"I'd like to know the answer to that," she said. "Am I his daughter?"

"No," answered Grice quietly. "If Grandson Gus is to be believed, you're a child of Blacker's only sister. She'd told him of the people who took care of you when you were young. That's how he traced you in New York. The old woman says that he fell in love with you." Grice broke off.

"Can't understand it," Rollison said, easily.

Grice forced a laugh. "You've got a lot to learn! Well, according to his wife, Blacker really made big money. He settled one half of his fortune on young Gus before his death, to avoid death duties. That was a complicated business but Mendelsohn's clerk says it was all quite legal.

Mendelsohn flew away because young Gus threatened to kill him if he didn't, not because of any guilt. But young Gus Blacker had one quality his grandfather didn't have. He's an inveterate gambler who takes big risks, and he lost most of his fortune. So he planned to get Miss Davenport's share."

Rollison said slowly: "It makes sense. Did Mrs Regson, *alias* Mrs Gus Blacker, ever try to make George believe that Mendelsohn was the villain?"

"Yes, she did—in order to try to send you after Mendelsohn and keep you on the wrong track."

"Most of Blacker's money would go to his grandson," mused Lola, as if she was listening only with half an ear.

"That's where it would have gone," Grice confirmed. He stood up. "One other thing you're bound to ask as soon as I've gone, too—why should young Gus kill the Moodys? They——"

"They must have known about the relationship between young Gus and Blacker," murmured Rollison, "or it could have been to frame me. I should say that old Gus planned to get me to the Manor and let me settle in, then have booby-traps and other unpleasantness started. That's why he left money to maintain the house if I spent some time there. But young Gus was in too much of a hurry—he wanted to finish the job in one go."

Grice grinned: "I can see you're really better, you think you know all the answers."

"And doesn't he?" asked Lola, sweetly. She stood up. "Won't you have another drink before you go, Mr Grice?" She moved to the corner cupboard. "I'm very anxious to know why young Gus attacked me so openly in New York—*was* that him?"

"Yes," answered Grice. "A man answering his description was seen at the wheel of the Chevrolet—and flew to England on the plane after yours."

"So that was it," said Lola.

She poured Grice a whisky and soda. He took it, said: "Thanks," and added:

"Gus himself hasn't talked at all, but his grandmother has told us everything she knows, or thinks she knows. It's all rather garbled, but the secondary purpose was simply to make sure that Rolly was looking two ways at once. Blacker left him the house, and left young Gus instructions about what to do, so as to get Rolly on the hop. Blacker revelled in the anticipation of what would happen, but he didn't anticipate that Gus would be in need of money. Young Gus reasoned that if Rolly had to concentrate on looking after you, he was likely to be more careless of himself. When you got here, you became the perfect suspect—that was the kind of irony which amused Grandson Gus as much as it would have amused Blacker. You simply became the bait."

"Delicious, too," murmured Rollison. "Delectable. I've never known bait like her. What about the girl with Gus, on the motor-scooter?"

"A dance-hall pick-up, whom he'd paid to swear he didn't go near the house, but she hadn't the nerve," answered Grice.

"Young Gus wasn't too clever," Rollison remarked. "What will you do with old Ma Regson, Bill?"

"She'll be tried as an accessory to capital murder," Grice said. "Young Gus will be hanged. There's no doubt that he murdered the Moodys, little doubt that Hanbury feared it, and rushed to the Manor to try to stop him. We've too many prints and too much specific evidence to put young Gus's guilt in any doubt. There may be a lot of legal complications, and I doubt myself whether the lawyers will have cleared this mess up until after the trial and the verdict. It'll take quite a time."

"Wonderful!" exclaimed Lola.

Grice looked surprised.

"Wonderful?"

"Rolly's going to have a house guest until I can leave
the country with all my money," declared Lola.

Grice chuckled.

They were laughing as they saw him out, and laughing
together as they came back into the big room. In the few
intervening moments, Jolly had cleared away ash trays
and glasses, and had dusted cigarette ash from the
desk.

"Will you be in to dinner, sir?" he inquired, obviously
with his tongue in his cheek.

"No, Jolly, we will not," declared Lola, and even
Rollison looked surprised. "We shall be in to supper, and
I am going to prepare it—and I won't require any help.
You are going over to Bill Ebbutt's place—he'll give you
a good dinner, won't he, Rolly?"

"If you say so," murmured Rollison.

"And you are going to tell Bill what Rolly was telling
me just before Grice arrived," declared Lola. "You are
going to tell him that the house Sandro Manor is going
to be run as a sanatorium for the poorer people of the East
End of London, or anyone in need, and that the money
which Mr Rollison inherited will go towards its upkeep.
The rest of the money needed will come from a little old
lady from Brooklyn. How about that, Richard?"

"Jolly," said Rollison.

"Sir," said Jolly.

"You've had your instructions."

"Very good, sir," said Jolly. "Before I go, may I make
one observation?"

"May he?" Rollison asked Lola.

"I'm not sure that I like you ribbing me," Lola said
but her eyes were laughing. "Sure, go ahead, Jolly."

"We received a cable while Mr Grice was here, from
Australia," Jolly said. "It announces that the gold lode
which Algoa Prendergast struck in the North Territories
of Australia was in fact a valuable one, and that considerable dividends can be expected from it. If some o

hose dividends could be allocated to the Sandro Manor
Sanatorium——"

"You can work that out for yourself," Lola said. "You
hurry and get ready, Jolly. I can't wait to get busy on
hat cooking stove."

THE END